For my brothers.
There's a little piece of all of you in every one of my Carson's
Bayou men.

Car Smarts

&

Bashful Hearts

KC Hart

BOOKS BY KC HART

Join KC's newsletter and receive a free ebook of Music Smarts and
Humble Hearts

PRAISE FOR KC'S BOOKS

Fresh Starts & Small Town Hearts

I was so impressed with KC's new book . . . *"I read it in two sittings. Her Cozy Mysteries were good, but now KC has found herself as an author and she has found her niché. Her writing seems so different . . . But in such a good way. She is a Christian romance author who is going places! Her characters are developed. I feel like I know them. They are human. They have real issues and real problems, with so much more depth than most romance stories. I found myself relating to their spiritual issues and relationship to God. KC's story will speak to many, with each seeing God's witness from their own needs. It's a MUST READ if you love flawed relationships with happy endings."* Author R Marshall Wright

Business Smarts & Reckless Hearts

Wonderful story... *"This is a great story of struggles, faith, belief in God, love and friendship. It is written in a way we can all relate to in some fashion. It's humorous, a little suspenseful, and the gospel is shared in a great way. I started reading it about midday and finished it before I went to bed. So entertaining that I couldn't put it down. Can't wait for the next one! Thank you, KC!"*

A Christmas Blaze

A Pure Delight... *"This is one of the sweetest stories I've read! From tragedy to triumph, it draws you into the lives of each character. Don't miss this one!"*

Elsie

Great story... *"This story was sweet and informative of the conditions of this time period. Loved the characters and the spiritual content. Another great one by KC and in a different genre from what she normally writes."*

Moonlight, Murder, & Small Town Secrets

"KC Hart tells the story with humor, wit, and the polite southern charm lacking in today's world. Keep an eye on KC Hart-she's good." Author R Marshall Wright

Music, Murder, & Small Town Romance

"A simple band competition turns into murder involving the local Casanova. This keeps you moving from one suspect to another without giving away the true villain. The dependence on God of the main character flows through the storyline in a very authentic way."

Memories, Murder, & Small Town Money

"I think this might be the best book in the series so far. The mystery is great, as usual, and kept me guessing until the end. I also really enjoyed seeing Katy's character grow and watch the sweet, honest friendship between her and Misty reach a new level. I highly recommend this book and the entire series."

Merry Murder & Small Town Santas

"A great murder mystery that will pull you in from the beginning. So fun trying to figure out who is the killer. The author keeps the reader on a rollercoaster ride with clues and suspects. The town

and characters are great fun and a little quirky. Katy is bold and gets herself into some situations that make her an excellent main character. I love reading this series and I'm looking forward to the next book. This is a clean book that doesn't have gore, but mystery and humor a plenty!"

Medicine, Murder & Small Town Scandal

"KC Hart gives hands and feet to a Christian way of life. KC Hart did it again. I love how her characters connect to my actual daily life. (Poor Katy, the struggle between chocolate pie and cholesterol!) I also love the way KC Hart makes belief in Jesus Christ an every day, every hour, every minute way of life, not something pulled out and shown off on "church" days or holidays.

Marriage, Murder & Small Town Schemes

"You will get engulfed in this awesome Christian cozy mystery by the very talented author, KC Hart. I loved it and would highly recommend this book and the entire series."

Mistaken Murder & Small Town Status

"Wow! Such an awesome book! I absolutely love that Christ is shared in Mistaken Murder & Small Town Status. This book kept me guessing until the very end. A definite must read. This is a great book to 'shoot the bull' about."

Mistletoe, Murder &Small Town Scoundrels

"Katy Cross delivers once again! She wove family life, small town ties, and finding God's purpose into a page turner and this one kept me guessing to the end."

CHAPTER ONE

*S*idney flipped the switch on the wall and looked around the cavernous garage with the concrete floors, hydraulic lift, tire storage racks, and enormous metal toolboxes. It finally belonged to him. Well, him and the bank. He had worked and put back for so long to own his own business. The dream was finally coming true. A slow, mellow smile crept across his face. It had been worth the wait.

Fiona's marriage in the spring left Sidney and Callie alone in Nana's old house. Without Fiona there nagging him to fix things, the home place was literally falling down around their ears. Nana's house was not on his priority list. For the past year, he had focused on his sisters and working to get enough money to start his business. The lack of concern for his home showed in the overgrown yard, saggy front porch, and brown spots on the ceiling in most of the rooms where he lived.

It had been a pain making sure Callie had enough of everything she needed for all of her high school clubs, sports, and activities, but it paid off in the end. Callie didn't love math like Fiona, nor was she valedictorian like her sister. She was smart enough, but her genuine talent was talking. The Lord had blessed Callie with the gift of gab, and she could sell ice cubes to an Eskimo. In the end, the debate team scholarship, volleyball scholarship, and the other smaller scholarships from the different clubs and activities, had allowed his baby sister to start college right on schedule this fall. It also paid for her dorm room and board. He breathed in the new smell of his place of business. All the long hours of working at Floyd's garage were starting to pay off. It was time to move forward and leave the past in the past.

Sidney's long legs strolled to the back of the garage, and he pulled open the door to the tiny office. A rackety old wooden desk took up the majority of the room along with a tall gray filing cabinet. The computer set alone on the desk, waiting to be put to work. The bare sheetrock walls would probably remain bare, except for a possible calendar. He didn't plan on spending a lot of time in the little office anyway. He had a good head for business. He and Fiona had that in common, but where Fiona thrived on figures and balancing the books, he loathed the entire process. No, he would eventually have to hire a secretary, and she could do what she wanted with the office walls. He would spend his days in the garage.

Honk, honk. Sidney closed the office door and hurried across the garage and out the side door to the gravel parking lot. He didn't officially open until tomorrow, but already had several jobs lined up. Maybe somebody saw his truck out front and decided to drop their vehicle by a day early.

"I thought we would find you here." Fiona Wade, Sidney's younger sister by eleven months, stepped out of the passenger's side of the shiny black Tahoe. "Have you started moving in yet?" She looked at the metal stairs going up the side of the building leading to the little one-bedroom apartment above the garage. "We figured you might need some help to get your mattress and bed frame up those stairs."

Sidney looked over his shoulder to his future home. The studio apartment had seemed like a great idea when he was building the garage. He had planned on moving in yesterday, but for some reason, the idea of leaving the family home, the place he had lived since he was five years old, brought on an unexpected wave of, what . . . nostalgia? "Yeah, I guess getting that old dresser and bed up there might be a two-person job. There's no hurry, though. I can do it a little at a time if I have to and just keep staying at the old house until it's done."

"While we're here, let's go ahead and get a load and bring it over," Fiona said, pushing her chestnut colored braid over her shoulder. "I want to see where you plan on putting everything."

"She's been rushing to get over here ever since we left church this afternoon," Langston, Fiona's husband, said. "She's really just being nosy and wants to arrange your furniture and stuff for you."

"That's right," Fiona said, arching an eyebrow. "He's my only brother and needs my help. If I don't help you." Fiona turned from her husband to Sidney and smiled. "You will keep everything shoved together and in boxes for the next five years."

Sidney patted his jeans pocket. "You're probably right." He pulled out the keys to his red double-cab Ford pickup. "Let's go load a few things."

"We don't have to if you don't want to, though." Fiona said, pulling on the handle of her Tahoe. "I don't want to be pushy or anything."

"Hmph," Langston snorted, "I think your brother knows you better than that."

"Hush, Lang." Fiona glanced from her husband to her

brother. "Until we find him a wife, I have to make sure he's taken care of."

Dream on, Sis. Sidney chuckled as he climbed into the cab of his truck, listening to his sister and brother-in-law swap words. They were so good for each other. Fiona was as hard-headed as a slab of granite. From an early age, she learned that as long as pain wasn't involved, Sidney pretty much let her do what she wanted where he was concerned. Things ran smoother that way, and it saved him a lot of arguing. Arguing turned his stomach.

Langston didn't seem to be bothered by her need to run things, but he didn't mind drawing a line in the sand when he felt it was necessary. Sidney had seen the man put his foot down a few times since they had married. It was kind of weird. Fiona had some kind of sixth sense and knew when she couldn't win an argument. She didn't bother fussing with Langston when that happened. She wasn't that way with Sidney or Callie; however. Sidney had walked away from his two sisters, going at it more times than he could count over the years. Both women could fuss until they were blue in the face, then turn right around and laugh and go about their business.

Sidney pulled out of the parking lot onto the street and looked in his rearview mirror at his sister. Fiona leaned across the seat and held Langston's face in her hands. Langston laughed and tugged against her grasp while she planted kisses on his cheeks. Sidney turned his eyes back to the road. Having someone in his life like that would have been nice. That melancholy feeling settled on his shoulders again. What was wrong with him today? Why was he dwelling on things he couldn't have? That type of dreaming was a waste of time.

He looked out the windshield at the orange and red leaves on the oak trees as he drove through town. The concrete statue of Carson the alligator, the town's mascot, stretched across the front lawn of the bank where Sidney had gotten his loan for his business. Decorating the alligator for Thanksgiving and then Christmas was a big deal. The kids around town loved to get their pictures made with the concrete mascot over the holidays. He sighed and turned his eyes back to the road.

No, family life wasn't in God's plans for him. If his business did as well as he projected it would, he could get the garage paid off in half the time of the loan contract. Then what? He stared out the windshield, seeing a future of him going downstairs to work on the wrecked or broken vehicles he loved so much every day for the next forty years. Alone. He eased down on the brake at the last stop sign and turned toward the street leading out of town to his old run-down house. Out his side window, a woman around his age stood in her little yard, raking leaves. A toddler played nearby on a blanket. A cat teased the curly-headed child with its tail. How did that happen? Did a guy just find the right girl and know she was the one? Was the next step marriage and a family? It was all such a big gamble. What if she wasn't the one? How did they know?

When Fiona started working for Langston, did she know he was the one? For a while, they acted like they were going their separate ways. Somehow, they had worked everything out and turned into the happy couple in the Tahoe behind him. He wouldn't ask his sister these kinds of questions. If he did, she would start trying to fix him up again. If he let her do that, he would go out with a girl and do something stupid and mess everything up and be embarrassed, just like all the other times. No, whatever everybody else seemed to have, that thing that let them know they had met the one, he didn't have it. That had become obvious. Best to stick to the role the Lord had laid out before him, friend and brother.

He slowed his truck and dodged a particularly nasty pothole. The roads got a lot rougher toward his home, but so did the houses. He pulled into the muddy dirt driveway in front of the ancient house he grew up in and watched Fiona and Langston pull in beside him.

"Sidney, you really need to mow." Fiona lifted the hem of her long gypsy skirt and waded through the sea of knee-high grass to the front porch. "I guess I can come by one day this week after I'm done with my classes and do it for you."

"No." Langston put a hand on Fiona's shoulder and stepped up the sagging porch step behind her. "You can't, and don't be picking up on anything heavy today or I will shut down this little moving venture so fast it will make your head spin."

Sidney watched Fiona reach up and get the house key from the rotting frame above the front door. "We don't have to do this today if you're under the weather, Fi. I can stay here just as easily as I can stay across town."

"I'm not under the weather," Fiona said, shoving open the front door. It creaked, scraping across the old hardwood floor. "We never got around to fixing those hinges, did we? I don't guess it matters now."

Sidney followed Fiona and Langston into the living room, flipping on the light switch. He looked around. A basket of clean clothes sat on the couch from his visit to the laundry mat yesterday, and a layer of dust covered the TV. Overall the place looked fairly neat, unlike the yard. "Y'all want a Coke or some tea?" Sidney asked, stepping around Langston, who had stopped in front of the old brown velvet couch with the wagon wheel arm rests. "I will have to borrow a dolly before we try to move the fridge or the dresser, but I think we can get the bed frame and mattresses."

"I'll take water." Fiona opened the olive-green fridge and

handed Sidney a Coke. "I don't want the baby to have the caffeine."

"Baby?" Sidney looked at Fiona and then back at Langston.

"Yes, brother-in-law," Langston said, his smile so wide it probably made his cheeks hurt. "I'm going to be a father. You're going to be an uncle."

CHAPTER TWO

$\mathcal{A}$delyn Jones looked in her rearview mirror at the four-year-old staring at her from the back seat. "We are almost there. Can you wait just a few more minutes?"

"I really gotta go, Momma." The little girl's body lurched forward, and she let out a scream. The car seat tilted, lunging from side to side. "Momma," she wailed, knuckles gripping the strap across her middle in a panic.

The car skidded across the road out of control and slammed into a skinny pine tree. The humongous deer that started the chain reaction limped off into the woods, disappearing from sight. Adelyn punched against the white, plastic airbag, suddenly shoving against her face. What happened? She had only glanced back at her daughter for a second. Where had the deer come from? How had she hit it so quickly? Zella's whimper drew her attention again to the back seat. "You okay back there, baby?"

"I peed my pants, Momma," the stubborn little green eyes glared at Adelyn, looking so much like her father. "Why did you make me pee my pants?"

"Oh, honey. It's going to be okay." She bit her lower lip

and looked back at her daughter. "We can change your clothes as long as you aren't hurt."

"I'm a big girl. I'm not supposed to have accidents." The child crossed her hands across her chest and tears dripped from her eyes. "It's your fault."

"You know what?" Adelyn unbuckled her seat belt. "You are exactly right. I'm the one who had the accident." She smiled a shaky smile. "Let me come around and get you out, then we'll see about getting you into some dry pants."

"You have a boo-boo." Zella pointed to the bloody gash on her mother's forehead.

A warm trickle ran down Adelyn's nose and she reached up, smearing the blood across her face. "Oh, it's not bad. Just a scratch." She reached over and grabbed the wet wipes from the glove compartment. "Can you sit there for a second and let me clean this up?"

"Hurry, Momma." The child's eyes stretched wide, staring at the blood flowing from Adelyn's head. "Are you gonna die?"

"No, baby. Momma's fine." Adelyn looked at the floor-board. Her purse, along with everything in it, lay scattered on the mat. She swallowed the lump of panic rising in her throat. Get Zella settled, call for help. But who to call? Not any of her friends from Shreveport. They were Zane's friends, too. If one of them let him know where she was, she would be in worse shape than she had been before. She was too far away for any of them to be able to help her, anyway.

"Momma, look." Zella pointed to a red truck pulling up beside the car. "That man can fix your boo-boo."

"Sit still, Zella." Adelyn pushed open her car door, the grass and underbrush pushing against her legs. "Let me see what we need to do."

*S*idney took a swallow of the hot, black coffee from his travel mug and yawned. Callie called at five-fifty-five, five minutes before his alarm clock went off, needing him to bring some books she had left at the house over the weekend. Fiona would be going to the college at ten, but Callie needed the books for her eight o'clock class.

"If I call Fi, she'll bring them, but she'll give me a lecture about gas prices and responsibility. Can you run them to me, Sid? Please?"

"I'll be there at six-forty-five. Don't make me wait for you. Today's opening day at the new shop, and I won't be late on my first day."

Callie was waiting when he pulled up at the dorms. He had not even had to get out of the truck. If he hurried, he would still make it back to town and get the garage open and have a few minutes to get settled before he raised the doors for business.

Sidney rounded a curve on the highway, heading back into town, and flipped down his visor, blocking out the morning sun. The black skid marks crossing from one side of the highway to the other had not been there when he had driven through earlier. He pressed his foot against the brake and rolled down his window. He searched the side of the road, his eyes following the black tire marks across the pavement to the muddy tracks in the ditch. A grey Honda Civic with the front caved in sat butted up against a splintered pine tree. Small trickles of steam rose from the hood. From the looks of things, the car had skidded across the road, spinning around and slamming into the little tree, but the front of the car had more damage than what the little tree had caused. The driver had hit something else too, but there were no other vehicles in either ditch.

Sidney pulled onto the shoulder of the road near the car

and climbed out of his truck. The car door creaked open, and a woman staggered out of the front seat, blood running down her face. "Hold on, ma'am. Let me help you."

"A deer ran out in front of us." The woman stood from the seat and leaned against the car. "We are okay." She paused and drooped backwards. "Just a little woozy."

"Hold on a second." Sidney ran the few feet to where the pale woman swayed, her knees buckling under her. "Looks like you need to sit down." He eased her back onto the edge of the seat. "Looks like you might need to go to the emergency room."

"No." The woman squeezed her eyes shut, then forced them open, the whites bright against the dark blue irises. "I'm fine. I just need to get the car going."

"Here." Sidney pushed the thick honey waves of hair back from the bloody cut on her forehead. "Let me take a look." He reached across her and grabbed the water bottle from the cup holder. "Do you have any napkins?"

The woman pulled a wad of McDonald's napkins from the console in the center. "Here. I promise it's not that bad. The bleeding's almost stopped."

Sidney wet the napkins and gently wiped the blood away from the cut along the woman's hairline. "It could probably use a stitch, but that's up to you."

"Are you gonna help us? I wet my pants."

Sidney looked past the woman to the back seat. "Well, hello there. I didn't see you at first." He flashed a grin at the little girl, black curly hair sticking out in all directions from her upturned face. "I'm not too good with wet pants, but I will see what I can do."

"I'm hungry too." The little girl looked at Sidney with serious eyes. "Momma said we could stop and get some chips."

"If you could help me get my car back on the road, that's

all we need," the woman said, smiling shakily at Sidney. "We are okay."

"You are in luck." Sidney pulled his hand back from her forehead and looked at the cut again. Blood oozed to the edges, and he pressed the napkin back in place. "I happen to own a garage and a tow truck. Let's get you two settled somewhere, then I'll come back and take care of your car."

"Yay!" The backseat passenger grinned. "And can I have chips?"

"Thank you, but I don't think." The woman reached up and took the napkin from Sidney's hand, continuing to hold pressure to the gash. "I don't think we can afford that right now."

"I hate to be the bearer of bad news, ma'am."

"Adelyn."

"Adelyn." Sidney smiled down at the pale woman. He looked at the strand of wavy hair clinging to her cheek. His fingers moved to rake it away, but her wide eyes and panicked expression brought him to his senses. "My name is Sidney. I live in Carson's Bayou just a few miles up the road. I'm afraid your car is not going anywhere like it is. Let me get you and the car settled. Don't worry about the cost right now."

"I don't guess I have much of a choice." Adelyn's eyes narrowed. "Okay, but I have my phone with me. I can call the police if . . ."

"If you would feel better, we can call the police first." Sidney's eyes softened, watching the woman's worried expression. "I don't want you to feel uncomfortable."

"Momma, I'm all wet and I need to go again."

"No, I guess we'd better go on with you."

"Okay." Sidney stepped back from the car's door and helped the woman out. "Wait right here. I'll get your daughter and we will get you two to town."

Adelyn reached in and hit the trunk button on the dash. "Do you mind grabbing that duffle bag?"

"I'll get it. If you can, go ahead and get in the truck." Sidney hurried around the back of the car and opened the door. He would have to hustle to make it to the garage before opening time. His first customer was arriving at eight to get the alternator looked at. He reached into the back and unbuckled the car seat. "We are right behind you."

"I'm not a baby." The little girl raised her arms up to Sidney. "I don't wet my pants anymore."

"I'm sure you don't." Sidney lifted the soggy child from the seat and perched her on his hip. "Hitting a deer would probably make me wet my pants too."

"Really?" The child's eyes followed Sidney's every movement. He slammed the car door and stepped around to the back to retrieve the duffle bag. "My name is Hazel May Jones," she said, looking down at her wet pants, and wrinkling her nose. "Momma calls me Zella."

"Hello, Hazel May Jones." Sidney slipped the duffle bag onto his free shoulder and hurried to the driver's door, the four-year-old hanging on to his other side. He reached in and locked the car, then headed to his truck where the woman was climbing in the passenger's side. "My name is Sidney Wallace Madison. My sisters call me Sid."

"You can call me Zella, and I'll call you Sid," the little girl said as Sidney passed her to her mother's lap. "But you can't call Momma Momma. That would be silly."

"I believe you are right." Sidney shut the passenger's door and glanced down at his wet shirt where the girl had left her mark on him. *What are you getting into, Sid? You don't have time for this.* He hurried around the front of his truck to his side of the vehicle, his work boots stomping down the briars and grass. He smiled at the girl and her mother through the windshield. "I have a bathroom in the apartment above the garage," he said, sliding behind the steering wheel. "You can change and rest up while I open my shop and take care of a few things. You can call your husband and let him know you're okay. I'll get your car to the shop in a bit and see what we can do for it."

"We are running away from Daddy."

"Zella." The woman put her hand over her daughter's mouth. "I'm sorry," she said, looking over at Sidney. "She is a chatterbox."

"It's okay." Sidney pulled away from the side of the road and started toward town. "It's not my business." The little girl pulled her mother's hand away from her mouth and he smiled. "Let's get you some chips." He turned his eyes to the woman staring at him. Something warm tugged at his heart. She looked so frightened, even as she wrapped her arms around her child like a protective momma bear. "Your business is your business," he said, compassion filling his voice. "Let's get you two settled. Then you can get in touch with whoever you need to. I won't ask any questions."

CHAPTER THREE

"*A*re you sure it's not an imposition?" Adelyn looked around the apartment. A set of regular sized bed springs, the ancient kind without a cloth covering, just metal coils, sat in the middle of the hardwood floor with a mattress on top. The bed frame and head and footboard set were propped against the nearby wall. A few cardboard boxes of various sizes sat around the edge of the room. Some had dishes and a few kitchen things, others towels and a hodge-podge of household items, and a few had clothes and bed linens. "I feel like I'm taking advantage of you."

"It's fine, really." Sidney walked across the room, weaving between the stuff on the floor to the kitchen area on the opposite wall. He set a Styrofoam covered plate with break-fast items on the tiny island bar near the sink and stove. "I'm going to be downstairs working for a few hours. Nobody will be up here. You might as well clean up Hazie May, eat breakfast, and chill out for a while. You both are probably beat. You two can kick back until I get my work done."

Sidney looked down at the little girl clutching her moth-er's hand with a vice-like grip. "There's stuff to drink, and that chocolate milk we were talking about over in the cooler." He winked at the child, and she grinned back attempting a wink of her own. "The bathroom's through those doors."

"Do you have bubbles?" Zella looked around the sparingly furnished room and wrinkled her brow. "I like to take bubble baths." She cut her eyes up to her mother, giving her the 'hush child' look. "I hate showers."

"Let's see what we can find."

Adelyn watched Sidney step over to a nearby box and start looking through its contents. "I can sit her in the sink and wash her off. Don't worry about us."

"Here you go. This stuff makes bubbles when I wash the dishes. I bet it will do the same thing in the tub. And what's this?" He pulled a half-empty bottle of shampoo out and set it by the breakfast plate. "I'm sure this will work."

"That will be perfect." Adelyn rolled her head on her shoulders. An ache thudded in the back of her neck. "You don't happen to have some Tylenol or maybe Advil or a BC powder, do you? I seem to be getting a little sore."

Sidney stepped over to another box with a couple of threadbare towels hanging over the edges. "Here's some ibuprofen pain relief." He shoved the towels to one side. "There's a bottle of peroxide and some bandaids in here too. You need to take care of that cut before too much longer."

"I will." Adelyn nodded her head. "Thank you again. My purse is still on the floorboard of the car, but I have a little money. I can give you some today and set up a payment plan for the rest. Only do the bare minimal. I don't care what our car looks like, as long as it runs and is safe."

"We can talk about that later." A horn tooted from the parking lot below. "There's Larry. I have to get downstairs. I'll check in on you later."

Adelyn watched Sidney's broad shoulders disappear through the door. Her mouth stretched into a deep yawn.

She slipped her hand from Zella's and stepped over to the waiting plate of food. "You gobble up your breakfast, and then we will give you a bath."

Zella ran across the room and looked through the long window down at the parking lot. "Don't call me Zella," she said, staring down at the man getting out of a truck. "Call me Hazie May. I like it better." She slowly turned and peered around at the boxes. "Can I wear my tutu?"

"Eat the eggs and bacon and you can put it on after your bath." Adelyn sat the ripped off lid of the to-go plate on the floor near the bed. "Now come say your blessing and eat. We have to get you out of those clothes and cleaned up."

"Sid said I was starting to smell like a barn full of cats." Zella looked down at her pink corduroy pants, damp from her earlier accident. "That's bad, I think." She started tugging down her pants.

"Hold on." Adelyn pulled a little box of chocolate milk from the ice chest sitting near an old white stove. She stepped over and helped her daughter strip down to her shirt and socks. She pulled a threadbare towel from one of the boxes. "Here. Wrap this towel around your bottom half until you finish breakfast and get in the tub."

Adelyn watched her daughter clasp her hands together and say her blessing over the food. She silently bowed her head. *Thank you, Lord, for protecting us this morning. Help me figure out what to do. I can't go back. You know that.*

An hour later, Adelyn slipped off the mattress where she had lain until Zella, now insisting on being called Hazie May, slept in a glittery purple tutu. She grabbed the duffle bag and stepped into the bathroom to shower. The ibuprofen helped the ache in her neck, but the soreness was getting worse. The hot water would help. It had helped the bruised muscles in the past. She squirted a blob of the red Suave shampoo and body wash into her palm and started massaging it into the honey brown waves, tangled with the blood from the cut. She must look a sight, probably worse than she felt, but it didn't matter. What mattered was coming up with a plan. Zane and their home were three hours behind her, thank goodness, but she was still an hour away from her parents' place. They didn't know she was coming, didn't know anything, so if she was delayed a day or two, it would be okay.

She finished up and stepped out of the shower into the compact, steamy bathroom. Her hand swiped a path across the fogged mirror, and she stared at the reflection looking back at her. She looked so tired, worn out. The past five years had drained away the confident woman she used to be. That strong, self-confident woman had to return if they were going to make it. She touched the tender gash on her forehead and scrunched her eyes. One thing at a time, Adelyn. Don't overwhelm yourself or Zella will suffer, and that must never happen. No matter what.

*S*idney slammed the hood on the truck and wiped his greasy hands on the rag hanging out of his coverall pocket. Three vehicles in the garage, and four waiting in the lot. It was going to be a productive day. Fiona was stopping by this afternoon when she finished her classes to write up receipts, call with estimates, and complete other office duties. One thing was sure, if the first day was any indication, he was going to have to hire a part-time secretary soon. With Fiona taking a few college courses, and now expecting a baby, it wasn't fair asking her to donate her afternoons to work for him.

He backed the truck out of the garage and parked it under the oak tree separating his building from the dilapidated sewing factory next door. This part of Carson's Bayou used to be the thriving industrial section back when his grandmother was young. She had worked at the sewing factory for years and years until it closed. Now the old building with the busted-out windows and overgrown parking lot was just an eyesore. Kind of like his old house. In a way, he was thankful for this. The abandoned building, probably full of asbestos insulation, had made the price of his lot one of the cheapest commercial properties in town.

He locked the truck and walked across the gravel parking lot to his next patient, a tan suburban needing its air conditioner checked. The sun beat down straight above his head, and he glanced at his watch. Eleven-fifty. He looked above the garage to the apartment windows. He would park this SUV and run to get his house guest's car with his refurbished tow-truck. Callie said the truck looked like Mater from some movie she had watched growing up. He wasn't sure if she meant it as an insult or a compliment, but it didn't matter. He didn't own the truck for its looks.

The woman, Adelyn, had been quiet on the way into town. Of course, he was no chatterbox himself, but he never had to say much living with his two sisters and grandmother. They could talk the hind leg off a mule. Not this woman. If it hadn't been for her daughter rattling on and on, the ride would have remained silent. Some of the woman's silence might have been from the shock of the accident. She had a nice goose egg on her head and a cut on her hairline that needed to be seen by a doctor.

He climbed out to the SUV and stepped into his office, hanging the keys to the truck and the SUV on a rack near the door. He let down the garage doors and stepped out the side, and started up the stairs to the apartment. The car was going to take a good bit of work. He would have to work on it at night so it wouldn't mess up his schedule for his customers that had delivered their vehicles that morning. That was okay. The woman needed a hand. This would be his good deed for the year. The preacher had done a sermon a while back on the good Samaritan. He didn't have any money to offer the woman, but he could offer his talent to fix her car. Something was going on with her. He didn't know what, and it was none of his business, but there was trouble in her life.

He reached the top of the stairs and rapped softly on the door. He wouldn't get involved in the woman's troubles. That would be a mistake. He had enough on his plate getting his business off the ground. He would fix her car. That would be the right thing, the Christian thing to do, so she could get on with her life.

The door opened, and a set of green eyes looked up at him. "Hey, Sid. I slept in your bed and used your bubbles. Smell my hair." The little girl tugged on his hands. "It smells like strawberries."

"I don't know if I should." Sidney leaned over and sniffed the shiny black curls. "I'm so hungry I could eat a whole patch of strawberries." He goosed the child under her arms, and she collapsed against him in a pile of giggles. "That sure is a fancy get-up you're wearing. Are you going to ride with me to get your car, or are you on your way to a ball?"

"I'm riding with you." Hazie May took a step back and twirled around in her purple tutu, complete with pink stockings and red cowboy boots. "I want to show you how I can dance when you're finished working."

"Zella." Adelyn stepped out of the bathroom.

"Hazie May, Momma." The little girl put her hands on her hips and looked over her shoulder. "I'm Hazie May now, not Zella."

"Oh, well, excuse me." Adelyn rolled her eyes, putting her hands on her hips, imitating the four-year-old. "Hazie May." She looked up at Sidney and stroked a strand of hair away from her cheek. "We are ready. Once I get my phone from the car, I can see about getting a hotel room. I don't want to keep bumming off you."

Sidney looked at the woman in the faded jeans and purple and gold LSU tee-shirt. Even with the swelling near her hairline, she was beautiful. A light spray of freckles across her nose matched the waves of honey colored hair falling across her shoulders. She was short, probably five-three, with great curves . . . and what was he doing? He jerked his eyes back to her face and smiled. "Let's get your car back to the shop and get something to eat. I'll call us something in at the Gumbo Hut and we'll pick it up on the way back. There's no reason to hurry about the rest."

CHAPTER FOUR

Sidney pulled back into the garage parking lot and stared as Adelyn slid out of the passenger's seat on the other side of the beat-up old tow truck. Hazie May looked at her mother, then back at Sid. She scooted toward him and stretched out her arms. He lifted her down to the ground. Adelyn picked up the plastic bag with their food and shut her door.

Sidney glanced at his watch. He needed to get back to work. "If you will hand me my plate, I'll eat down here," he said, as Adelyn rounded the corner of the old truck. "Y'all can go back upstairs if you want to."

"We want to eat with you, Sid." Hazie May looked up, her words tumbling rapidly from her lips. "Don't we, Momma?"

"We need to get out of Mister Sidney's way," Adelyn said, frowning down at her daughter. "We will go upstairs like he said, so he can get to work."

"But Momma . . ."

"You can eat down here with me if you want to," Sidney said, tousling the little girl's hair. "You won't be in the way at all. I'm here by myself, so there's nobody you can bother. I just figured you wouldn't want to eat in a garage."

"See, Momma. Sid." Hazie May looked at her mother's warning eyes. "I mean, Mr. Sidney wants us to eat with him."

"Are you sure?" Adelyn's eyes narrowed. "I don't want to be in your way."

"I'm sure. Why don't you run upstairs and get us some drinks from the ice chest while I get our food set up? Hazie May can show me those dances she's been talking about while we eat."

"Please, Momma." Hazie May stuck her bottom lip out and looked up at her mother's indecisive face.

"Okay," Adelyn said, letting out a sigh. "I can see you two are ganging up on me. Zell . . . I mean Hazie May, you come wash your hands first though."

"But . . ."

"That's a deal breaker, young lady. Clean hands or no food."

Hazie May looked at her mother, her eyebrows pulling low. "Okay, I'll be right back, Sid." She stomped off toward the stairs.

"Your hands are full." Sidney said, taking the bag of food from Adelyn.

"You have no idea," Adelyn said, shaking her head. "She's four going on twenty-four. Are you sure this is okay?"

"It's fine. As a matter of fact, I will enjoy the company." Adelyn turned and headed toward the stairs. Sidney smiled. He unlocked the side door and stepped into the garage, flipping the fluorescent light on as he entered. The company would be a nice change. Things had gotten awful lonely in the old house now that his sisters were gone.

Sidney walked to the back of the garage and looked around. Several industrial sized metal toolboxes lined the back wall. He could roll one of them out to put the food on. Or they could cram into the tiny office to eat. He set the bag on one of the toolboxes and hurried back outside to his truck. The old quilt from behind the seat would make a perfect picnic blanket. He walked back inside and looked around the concrete floor for a place to eat, whistling as he unfolded the quilt. *What are you doing, Sidney? This is not you. You have work to do, and this woman and her child are not your problem.*

Sidney stepped over and grabbed the Gumbo Hut bag, ignoring the voice of reason that had kept him safe since childhood. One day. This was just one day, not a long-term commitment. He was not obligating himself to anything, well, except fixing the car, and he hadn't said anything to Adelyn about what he was considering yet, anyway. He would eat lunch, feel her out a little. If she had a plan to get back on the road and get to where she was going, fine. He would keep his mouth shut and let her tend to her own business. If she really needed his help, he ran his hand along his jawline, if she really needed his help, he had to do the right thing. He would just do the right thing from a distance.

"Knock, knock."

Adelyn and Hazie May walked through the side door and Sidney looked up. "Back here," he said, straightening the corner of the blanket. "I was able to reserve us the best seat in the house."

"I have Yoo Hoo, Dr. Pepper, or water." Adelyn put the drinks down on the blanket and sat down. Hazie May sat beside her, a chocolate milk box in her hand.

"Hmm, tough choice." Sidney sat down on the other side of the blanket and pulled out the boxes of food. "You choose first. I can drink whatever."

"Momma loves Dr. Pepper," Hazie May said, ripping the

plastic from her straw with her teeth. "She won't let me have but a sip though."

"I think I'll take the water, although that Yoo Hoo is mighty tempting." Sidney peeked in the to-go box and passed the shrimp poor-boy across to Adelyn. "My Nana didn't let us have Cokes either. I grew up on Kool-aide, tea, milk, and water."

"Whose Nana?" Hazie May jabbed the straw into the foil covered hole in the top of the milk box with practiced accuracy. "Nana sounds like banana, doesn't it?"

"Hazie May." Adelyn sat her plate beside her and took the second plate Sidney passed across the blanket. "What did we talk about upstairs?"

Hazie May's lips turned down. "I'm not asking too many questions, Momma, only one."

"Nana was my grandmother." Sidney took the last Styrofoam plate from the box and set it in front of him. "She raised me and my two sisters." He took the sweaty bottle of water Adelyn passed to him. "Let's say the blessing before my stomach starts sounding like a beached whale."

Hazie May grasped Sidney's hand and then her mother's. "I can say it."

The little girl prayed God is grape, God is good, followed by a brief thank you for her chocolate milk, chicken strips, and fries. Sidney lifted his head and grinned when she said amen. God is grape was a version of the childhood prayer he had never heard before. It would be interesting to find out her thoughts on the Creator. She was probably a handful of questions during Sunday school. Hazie May opened the box of food and picked up a fry. She reminded him of Fiona when she was little, opinionated, and vocal.

"Where was your mamma?" Hazie May asked, licking a glob of ketchup from her fry. "Nana's a funny name."

"I lived with my Nana. She is the one who raised me."

"Why? Didn't you have a momma?"

"Hazel May Jones." Adelyn's cheeks flushed bright red. "It's time for you to hush and eat your lunch." Adelyn looked over at Sidney and fumbled with opening her bottle of Dr. Pepper. "I'm sorry. She doesn't normally take to strangers the way she's taken to you."

"I don't mind talking, if you don't mind." Sidney pulled the top bun from his hamburger and removed the pickles.

"Well, if you get tired of answering questions, tell her to hush." Adelyn raised half of the poor-boy to her mouth. "Thank you for lunch. This will be enough for us to have at supper too."

"Did you have a momma?" Hazie May asked again, not put off in the least by her mother's correction.

"I did, but I moved in with my grandmother when I was a little bit older than you."

"We are going to my grandmother's house." Hazie May dipped the same soggy fry back in the ketchup and raised it to her lips. "I've never been there before, but Momma says she has a pool."

"Sounds like a great place." Sidney took a bite of his burger and grinned as the child licked the ketchup off for the second time. He turned his gaze to Adelyn. "I have to work on the cars already on the schedule for the rest of the day, but I'll start on yours tonight. You might want to call your parents and have them come get you. I can contact you when I have your car ready."

"No." Adelyn bit her lower lip and her eyes darted around the room. "Actually, my parents don't know we're coming. I think I'll find a hotel tonight and leave after you are finished tomorrow." She looked back at Sidney. "If I call them, they will worry. Is there a Super Eight or something like that around here?"

"We have one hotel here in town." Sidney looked at

Adelyn's worried expression. "I hate to mess up your plans, but it's going to take a few days to fix your car. I've got to bend out the front bumper so you can turn the wheel, and I won't know what's going on under the hood until I have a look."

Adelyn's shoulders slumped, and she laid the sandwich back on her plate. "I, um. I've only got a couple hundred dollars." She looked down at the blanket, and then over at Hazie May. "I'm not sure what to do. Is there a car rental place around anywhere?"

Sidney put down his burger and picked up a paper napkin to wipe the grease from his fingers. "I'm afraid not, but listen. Nobody is staying in the upstairs apartment." He watched as she lifted her eyes. Hope and fear mixed on her face. He shouldn't get involved. This was not his problem. "You two can stay there until I get your car fixed."

"How can I . . ." Adelyn paused, glancing over at her daughter. Hazie May took a long pull from her chocolate milk carton as she picked a piece of fallen chicken strip from the folds of her tutu. "Is there anything I can do to repay you? Like clean your house, or, I don't know, anything? I just don't know." Her voice faded, and she ducked her head again. She took a deep breath and lifted her chin, her voice back in control. "If there is some way I can earn our keep, that will work fine."

Sidney looked across the blanket. The consequences of his words didn't matter. At least, they didn't matter as much as what he was seeing. This beautiful woman needed a place to stay, and he had a place. He was not a cold-hearted monster. "You can help me in the office and help set the apartment up. As a matter of fact, if you can do those two things, you will actually be doing me a favor."

"I doubt that," Adelyn said, picking up a fry and nibbling the end. "You are being nice." She dropped the fry back on the plate. "Right now, I'm between a rock and a hard place. I will do whatever needs doing if you will let us stay until you fix the car."

"Then it's a deal." Sidney's phone buzzed, and he pulled it from his pocket. "Excuse me a second." He stood and stepped over to the office door a few feet away to talk to Fiona. After a couple of minutes, he put his phone back in his pocket and walked back to the blanket.

"I ate your pickles," Hazie May said, grinning at Sidney as he sat back down. "I like pickles a lot."

"From now on, I will save all my pickles for you." Sidney picked up his burger and looked over at Adelyn, sipping on the Dr. Pepper, her food uneaten. "My sister and brother-in-law will be over after while, and we will move the fridge and a few more things over here. Can you cook?" He took a bite of his burger, peering at her from under hooded eyes.

"I can cook as long as you don't want anything fancy," Adelyn said, passing a napkin to Hazie May. "Here, honey, you have ketchup on your cheek." She looked back at Sidney. "Why?"

"I'm thinking you can save me a good chunk of change. If you can cook our meals, I won't have to eat out while I'm here at work. I go to the Gumbo Hut almost every day at lunchtime, or either eat a jerky stick and just tough it out. A lot of evenings I either grab something from the gas station deli or eat a frozen pizza. If you make the meals while you are here, that will save me from having to buy all my food from those places."

"I can definitely do that." Adelyn leaned over and swiped her thumb across her daughter's cheek, wiping away the ketchup the child had smeared with the napkin. "But how long do you think we will be here?"

"Maybe a couple of days, but it could be a week or a little

more. It's according to what I find, and how long it takes to get the parts to fix the problems."

"Oh." Adelyn's eyes narrowed. "Well, I might need to tell you a couple of things if we have to stay that long. Just to be safe."

CHAPTER FIVE

"Uh, sure." Sidney glanced over at Hazie May, who was suddenly extremely interested in their conversation. "When do you want to talk?"

"Hazie May." Adelyn turned to her daughter. "Do you want to watch Peppa Pig on my phone?"

"I want to listen to you and Sid," Hazie May said, chin firm. "I can watch Peppa Pig later."

"How about you go watch Peppa Pig now, like I want you to? Then we will go upstairs in a bit and start pulling stuff from Mr. Sidney's boxes like you wanted to earlier."

"Can't I sit here with you and then look at Sid's stuff, too?" Hazie May stretched her eyes wide. "Please, Momma."

"If you go and let me talk to Mr. Sid a minute like a good girl, we will go look at his stuff. If you don't do as I'm asking, you will sit in the corner while I talk to Mr. Sid anyway. No Peppa."

"Okay." Hazie May drug the word out like she had just received a prison sentence, and her lips pushed into a frown. "I'll watch Peppa."

"Good girl." Adelyn slipped her phone from her pocket and began pulling up the cartoon.

"If you be good and help your mother straighten up while I work down here, I will give you five dimes tonight at dinner," Sidney said, looking at Hazie May's face. "How does that sound?"

"Five dimes?" Hazie May looked up at Sid, lips poked out. "Is that enough for a toy?"

"Probably not," Sid said. "But if you are good and help your mother each day, I will give you five dimes every evening. By the weekend, you will have twenty-five dimes."

"Whoa." Hazie May stood up and a sprinkle of food crumbs showered the blanket. "That's a ton of money." She stepped over and flung her arms around Sidney's unexpecting neck, almost toppling him over. "Thank you, Sid."

"You are welcome." Sidney put one hand behind him to prevent falling over backwards and patted the child's back with the other. When was the last time someone hugged him with such abandon? His sisters hugged him, but it seemed more out of habit. He looked across the pallet at Adelyn. Her eyes narrowed. "Okay, Miss Priss." He pushed the child away from his chest. "Get your mom's phone, and get to watching this peppermint pig."

"Peppa Pig." Hazie May stepped across the pallet and took the phone from her mother's hand. "Peppermint pig is silly."

*a*delyn settled Hazie May in the far corner of the garage with the cartoon on the phone and a bottle of Yoo Hoo. The sugar from the chocolate milk, and now the chocolate drink, would have the child bouncing off the walls in the afternoon, but she would deal with that later. Right now, she had to deal with the man waiting for her on the blanket. How did the plan she had worked so hard to make happen get messed up so easily?

She pulled in a deep breath and straightened her shoulders. A new back-up plan was required. She turned and walked back to the blanket. This plan would work. She just needed to lay down a few ground rules. Sidney Madison seemed like a nice guy, but then again, so had Zane five years ago when they met.

"My daughter has really taken to you." Adelyn sat back down on the blanket and looked at the man across from her. His chocolate colored curls stuck out this way and that, giving him a boyish charm, but his broad chest and deep voice had no hint of boyhood in them. "I need you to understand that, if I have to, I will do anything for my child." She caught his eyes with hers and held them. "I have been hurt before by people I thought I could trust, but my daughter hasn't. I plan on keeping it that way. Do I make myself clear?"

"Crystal." Sidney stared back, not breaking eye contact. "I don't know what you are running from, but I can probably guess. I'm not trying to get tangled up in your affairs, and I definitely do not mean you or your daughter any harm."

"Okay." Adelyn studied Sidney's face, looking for deception. "I'm not ungrateful, but I have to be careful." She turned her eyes to the corner where her daughter sat. "For her sake."

"I understand." Sidney followed Adelyn's gaze. "I would be the same way. You will see. You can trust me. I'm trying to be a friend, that's all. No strings attached. If I'm reading your situation correctly, I was in Hazie May's shoes when I was a little bit older than her, except my momma didn't stick around." He turned and looked back at Adelyn. "I don't want that to happen to her . . . to you. I'm trying to do the right thing, that's all."

"My ex-husband, he's made it unbelievably hard on me over the last several months." The memories flooded

Adelyn's mind and her stomach knotted. "Last week when I went to pick my daughter up from daycare, he was waiting for us in the parking lot. He's not supposed to see her, be near me, unless we are supervised." A shudder ran across the back of her neck. "Here lately, he seems to think those rules are suggestions."

"That's why you left town?" Sidney's voice lowered. "You're scared he'll take Hazie May?"

"That's one of the reasons." Adelyn tugged on the neck of her tee-shirt. "I needed to put some distance between us. Even Shreveport was too small for us and him. I left early this morning, the middle of the night really, but he probably knows something's up by now. Last week, after he approached us at the daycare, he started waiting across the street for us to come out of the house every morning. I knew he was planning something, so I grabbed a few things and we left town." She reached up and gently touched the band aide at her hairline. "He has no rights to her, so I'm not breaking any laws."

"You are protecting your child." Sidney pulled in a deep breath and Adelyn eyed him as something flickered across his face, then disappeared. "Will your parents help you?"

"I, uh." How much should she tell this man? He was going out of his way to help her. She had to believe that the Lord had put him in her path for a reason. But still. "I'm not sure. I didn't leave on the best of terms last time I saw them."

"Oh."

He didn't say anything else, didn't ask any questions. Good. If he didn't ask, she wouldn't tell. "I don't think Zane will find us, but still, I need to be careful. If you will keep my business to yourself while I'm here, I will do whatever you need doing until we can be on our way. Once I get some- where and find a job, I will pay you what I owe you for the car."

"I won't say anything to anybody. If anyone asks, you are my new secretary." Sidney's jaw set firm as he looked over at the four-year-old. "That's all anybody needs to know."

The knot in Adelyn's gut eased a little, and she blew out a breath of air. "Thank you. This was not the plan, but I am running low on options."

"Don't worry. Both of you will be safe here." Hazie May giggled from the corner where she was absorbed in the cartoon. "I promise you that."

"So, she hit a deer, wrecked her car, and you offered her your apartment and a job?" Fiona's eyebrows raised. "What's going on, Sidney? This is not like you."

"Don't worry about it, Sis. I needed a secretary, and one practically fell into my lap. You should be happy. Now you won't have to help me out. You can concentrate on school and the baby and your husband." Sidney looked in the fridge one more time, then closed the door. "Where did Langston go? I'm ready to get this thing on the truck and get back to the garage."

"He's on the porch. His brother called." She looked around the tiny kitchen at the open cabinet doors, shelves empty, boxes of food sitting on the counter. "I don't understand how you expect to live here without a refrigerator or food, though."

Fiona walk through the kitchen, into the living room, and out the front door. If Sidney could keep the details from her about why Adelyn was moving in, he could keep them from anybody. He looked around the kitchen. She was right. This was not like him, and what he was doing made him want to shut the front door and lock everybody out, including Adelyn and her daughter. The sight of Adelyn peeking out of his bathroom this morning, of Hazie May in her purple tutu, flashed through his mind, and the clenching in his gut relaxed. No, he had to do this. What if Nana had turned his mother away? What if his mother had dragged him and his sisters back to the man who had bullied her? He hadn't thought of that day in a long time. A memory of his father screaming at his mother pushed its way from somewhere in the back of his mind.

"Don't yell at my mother!" He was five when he finally got the courage to take on his father, kicking him in the shin, punching him in the groin. To his amazement, the man had doubled over like a bowling pin. When he got back up, the anger in his eyes had burned a mark on Sidney's soul he had never forgotten. He hid behind his mother. His father had stormed out, and everything seemed okay. But it wasn't. A week later, he met his Nana and never saw his mother again.

"No. This was the one time he couldn't walk away. Adelyn was worried about going back to her parents. There was something going on there that she wasn't telling, but it didn't matter. Hazie May needed her mother, and her mother needed him. Not forever, just for the next week or two. He could do the right thing for a couple of weeks. Really, what was it costing him, anyway? A little night work, a few car parts? He wrapped a bungee cord around the refrigerator and secured it close as the front door opened again.

"Alright, man," Langston said, pushing in the dolly. "Let's get this stuff on your truck. Lucas is meeting us at your garage to get everything up the stairs."

"You didn't have to call your brother." Sidney leaned into the fridge, tilting it enough for Langston to slide the dolly into place. "I'll get everything in the apartment—somehow."

"We are family. That's what we do." Langston slapped Sidney on the back as his voice took on a serious tone. "Look, man, I don't know what's going on with this woman and her kid, but unlike my wife, I'm not going to pry. You are a grown man and one of the most level-headed people I have ever met." He pulled down slowly on the dolly as Sidney lowered the fridge to be rolled out the front door. "If you need me, though, I'm here for you."

"Thanks." Sidney looked at Langston, grateful for his friendship and trust. "I have everything under control, but it's good to know you have my back."

"Always, brother-in-law. All you have to do is call."

CHAPTER SIX

*A*delyn adjusted the seat belt in Sidney's truck across her chest. She moved it a little lower, so it didn't rub against her collarbone. Her chest no longer felt sore from the crash, but the belt rubbed her the wrong way. So far, the move into Sidney's apartment had gone well, except for a few minor mishaps like burning the toast, smoking up the apartment, setting off the fire alarm, and having the fire department show up. No biggie. Who kept a toaster that didn't pop up? Sidney Madison, that's who. He said he was planning on fixing it when he got around to it. He had tucked it away downstairs in the garage on a shelf where the next unsuspecting soul wouldn't torch the place.

Two weeks had flown by. Sidney and Hazie May had taken to each other like two peas in a pod. A soft smile settled on Adelyn's face. Her little girl had gone from being Zella to Hazie May, and there was no turning back. Adelyn didn't mind, liked it, actually. Hazel was her father's sister's name, and Hazie May was her namesake. Aunt Hazel had been more like a grandmother to Adelyn than an aunt, and sometimes, often times, more like a mother as well. Adelyn hadn't told all of this to Zane. He wouldn't have cared why she wanted to name their child the "archaic" name anyway. He wasn't too happy that she filled out the birth certificate without him. For once in their relationship, she had stuck to her guns, and Hazel May Jones remained her sweet girl's name.

Zane refused to call their girl Hazel, or let Adelyn either, and the name Zella had developed. Just another way he had of controlling and manipulating every decision she had ever made. Adelyn picked up the bottle of Dr. Pepper from the drink holder and took a sip. That life was finally over. No going back, no matter how today went. Sidney had wanted to come with her today, but she needed to be alone when she met her parents. Her father would be happy to see her, but there was no telling how her mother would react. She didn't want anyone around in case things went south, especially Hazie May.

Adelyn's fingers gently rubbed the scab at the top of her forehead. Leaning on Sidney Madison was such an easy thing to do, but she could not get used to it. Leaning on a man was why she was in the shape she was in now. Of course, Sidney was polar opposites from Zane in every way. Even though she was working for him to pay off everything he was doing for her, he always hung around after they were through eating and helped wash the dishes. Yesterday afternoon it was either go to the laundry mat or wear dirty clothes. Instead of telling her where to go, they had waited until the garage closed. He had run to his house and grabbed his laundry, packed hers down the stairs to the truck, and taken them there, making sure he did all the lifting and toting. She was definitely not used to that. The thing that surprised her the most occurred while they were waiting on the clothes. Instead of zoning out and playing on his phone, he played with Hazie May and talked to Adelyn. He didn't pry, that didn't seem to be his nature. He just told her little things about himself, how he liked Snickers more than Butterfingers. He preferred to sit close to the back in church so he could get out after the service before his sisters or the women of the congregation had a chance to try to fix him up with their latest woman of the hour. Little things like that. She smiled again and drained the last swallow from the Dr. Pepper bottle.

A warm feeling filled her chest as his smiling face filled her mind. His chocolate curls, blue eyes, and five o'clock shadow made such a handsome combination, even in his greasy coveralls and work boots. Last night, after they finished chicken with peas and cornbread, he returned to the garage, like every evening, to work on her car. Hazie May, freshly bathed and in a purple nightgown complete with unicorns and rainbows, insisted on going downstairs to tell him goodnight before getting in bed. Sidney had rolled out from under the car and patiently listened as Hazie May explained the difference between an orange cat with brown stripes and a brown cat with orange stripes. He then rode her on his shoulders back upstairs to the bed and tucked her in. Watching him kneel beside her when she said her prayers, and then kissing her forehead, had choked Adelyn up. Sidney spent more time with her daughter in the past two weeks than the child's own father spent in her entire lifetime.

Adelyn adjusted the seat belt again and turned into the neighborhood where she grew up, the neighborhood she had not seen in over five years. The upper middle-income houses lining both sides of the street hadn't changed much. The yards looked manicured, and the sidewalks were free of clutter. She pulled the big red truck into the driveway of the home on the corner, behind the Cadillac SUV in the garage. Good, someone was home. Hopefully, it was her father, but either way, this had to be done.

She flipped down the visor and ran her fingers through the top of her hair, pulling a few wisps over the scab. It wasn't terribly noticeable. The past five years had changed her from the headstrong girl who stormed out of this house that night. She would have to be humble, ask forgiveness, and rely on her father's mercy and cool head. One of her greatest regrets was cutting her father out of her, and Hazie May's lives. Unfortunately, to get Father, you had to take Mother. She swallowed down the worry creeping up her throat. She must do this for Hazie May. *Lord, please give me courage to face Mother. Please help me say the right things.*

Adelyn knocked on the front door, the LSU Tigers door hanger proudly displayed for visitors to see. Both of her parents graduated from the university. They expected their only child to do the same. She did okay the first two years, keeping a low B average. Mother held her tongue. When she came home halfway through her third semester with Cs and even a D, Mother exploded. When Adelyn announced she was changing her major from electrical engineering to elementary education, she might as well have said she was moving to Bourbon Street to panhandle for the rest of her life.

"You will either be poor as a church mouse and barely scrape by, or you will be dependent on someone else to pay your bills," Mother said, anger flashing from her eyes. "Either one is not acceptable. I have sunk too much time and money into securing your future to have you mess it up now."

"It's my future, Mother." A familiar knot formed in Adelyn's stomach as the memory of their last conversation flashed into her mind. "I cannot do what you are asking me to do. I've tried, I really have, but it's not me."

She packed a bag that afternoon and drove away. If she hadn't, her mother would have forced her to return to the classes she would eventually fail. She would force her to take them and retake them, whatever it took to get that degree, and then work at a job that would choke the life out of her. A life that her mother could proudly chat about at her civic club. Father had given her a credit card and an envelope full of cash as she slipped out the door. For two months, she lived on the money and used the card until she got a job as a teaching assistant for an elementary school in Shreveport.

Her mother was right about one thing. She had been poor —until she met Zane. The perfect man with the perfect job, perfect income, perfect marriage . . . the oral surgeon. The slap when she innocently called him a dentist was the first of many to come in their marriage. On the outside it was perfect, but behind closed doors when they were alone, things had fallen apart in a hurry.

Adelyn pulled in a deep breath, forcing her thoughts back to the present. The door opened and the woman who she dreaded seeing stared at her, not a hair out of place, make-up flawless.

"Adelyn."

"Mother." Adelyn opened and closed her hands at her side, careful not to wring them. Wringing hands drove her mother nuts. "Can I come in?"

"Of course." Mrs. Swan stepped to the side, then looked into the yard as Adelyn entered. "Are you alone?"

"Yes, ma'am. Is Father here."

"No. He's not here." Mrs. Swan shut the door behind them and led Adelyn to the living room. "Sit. Let me make a call and cancel an appointment. After that, we will talk."

Adelyn opened her mouth to tell her not to change her plans, but remained silent. She looked around the room. Most things seemed the same. Her graduation photo still hung over the fireplace. The large family photo in the fancy gold frame still hung over the sofa. There wasn't a speck of dust anywhere, as usual. Something was different, though, but what? She scanned the room. What?

"Now." Mrs. Swan stepped back into the room and sat on the love seat. Her rust-colored A-line cotton dress and chocolate colored cardigan fit her thin frame perfectly. She tilted her trim tanned legs to the side and crossed her ankles. "Why are you here?"

Mother was being mother. She couldn't help it any more than a lizard could help being scaly. At least, that's what Adelyn decided to believe. If she believed anything else, she would run to the door and never look back. The thing that baffled her was, why had Father married Mother in the first place? Then again, she was the pot calling the kettle black. Zane. That's who he reminded her of, Mother. She had always known there was someone that Zane Jones made her think of. She just couldn't figure out who it was. Sitting here, under the scrutiny of the perfectly chiseled icy glare of the woman who raised her, it all became clear. Could she actually be thinking of bringing her daughter under the influence of a woman she had finally escaped when she was twenty-one years old? Her heart started pounding in her chest. Her hands came together, rubbing methodically in her lap.

"Well?" Mrs. Swan raised an eyebrow and stared down at Adelyn's hands, then back at her face. "I cancelled an important appointment, Adelyn. Are you going to explain what you are doing here?"

"Where's Father?" Adelyn forced her hands apart and back to her side. She would talk to Father, see if he could help her, but moving back to this house, that would be a disaster. What had she been thinking? "I need to see Father."

"Your father passed away last year. I had no way of getting in touch with you, and honestly, Adelyn. If you truly cared about him, or me, you would not have disappeared off the face of the earth the way you did."

"He's dead?" The words hit Adelyn like ice cold water in the face. Of all the scenarios that played through her mind as she prepared for the trip over here, this was not one of them. "What—how did he die?"

"Car accident." Mrs. Swan lifted her chin and looked down her nose at Adelyn. "Killed instantly. Everyone could not believe you didn't come. But . . . I did the best I could with the situation." She looked down and picked an invisible piece of lint from her dress. "Now, again. What do you want?"

Adelyn stood and glanced around the room. His recliner, the worn leather one that Mother despised. Daddy's recliner was gone. "Nothing, Mother. Call your friend or whoever that was back. You can keep your important meeting."

CHAPTER SEVEN

Sidney unwrapped the biscuit, strawberry jam squishing from the sides, and passed it across the picnic table to Hazie May. "I'm not sure what else there is to do around here besides the park," he said, looking at the little girl decked out in her red and white checked jumper, white tights and the ever-present cowboy boots. "We might go by the library when we run out of things to do here. I think there used to be a jumpy house somewhere around town, but I don't know if it's still open or not. I'm kind of out of touch with kid stuff."

"That's okay, Sid. Can I ride on the merry-go-round?" Hazie May asked, twisting around and looking at the playground equipment in one area of the park several yards away. "My school didn't have a merry-go-round."

"Sure can." Sidney unwrapped his own biscuit and opened his container of milk. "Let's get some breakfast in our bellies, then we will check it out." He bowed his head, and the child said her blessing over their food. He passed her a chocolate milk box.

"I wish Momma could have come with us. She loves being

outside." Hazie May took a bite of the biscuit, and a cascade of crumbs fell onto her jumper. "She looked sad today. I think it's because she wanted to go with us instead of going to see her momma."

"Probably so, but don't worry. We can bring her back here with us soon."

"Today?" Hazie May licked a glob of jam from the bottom of the biscuit. "She said she would be back after lunch. We might come back again. I bet that would make her smile real big."

"I doubt she will want to come today." Sidney grinned at the strawberry jam sticking to Hazie May's cheek near her lips. "Maybe tomorrow after church. Here." He passed a napkin across the table. "You have breakfast on your cheek."

"Sid." Hazie May took the napkin and wiped her cheek. Her eyes narrowed and thoughts ran through her head. "When we leave to go live with my new pawpaw, will you come visit us?"

Sidney picked up his carton of milk and took a long drink, not saying a word. How should he answer that? He was getting attached to Adelyn and Hazie May. It was obvious, but all of this was temporary. Adelyn had seemed to put off going to talk to her parents until the last minute, almost like she was dreading it. He hadn't asked any questions. It wasn't any of his business. She said she planned to stay with her folks until she was able to get back on her feet.

He was about done with the car, and their time together would soon be over. He had scrounged around and found parts at the junk yard instead of ordering new ones to keep the repair costs as low as possible. That's how he had gotten his red truck. He bought it cheap after a high school kid totaled it out and brought it to Floyds, where he used to work. He worked on it, fixing one thing at a time with salvaged parts from the junkyard. It took longer, but he couldn't afford a nice truck any other way. Doing Adelyn's repairs the same way had extended their stay another week, and every day they stayed was one more day that he was getting more attached.

Now the car was about ready. Adelyn and Hazie May would be moving away. Where did he fit into that? Nowhere, really. He would go back to doing his thing, and they would get on with their lives. "Hmm. You know I stay pretty busy in that garage all day working."

"Well, if you can't come see us, can we come see you?" Hazie May's brow furrowed. "I don't want to go live with my pawpaw if we can't come back and visit."

"You can come visit me whenever you want to." Sidney leaned across the table and patted Hazie May's hand. "Don't you worry about it, okay?"

"Okay." She picked up her drink box and took another pull on her straw as she stared across the park, pondering what he had said.

"Excuse me." A woman, probably in her fifties, in walking shorts and a tee-shirt, stepped up to their picnic table. "Are you in that tow truck? Another lady said she thought it was yours."

"Yes, ma'am." Sidney smiled politely. "Can I help you with something?"

"I hope so. My car won't start." She turned and pointed to a blue Toyota parked in the nearby lot. "My doctor said I need to walk every day to get my cholesterol down, or he was going to put me on pills. This is my third morning to walk, and wouldn't you know it? My car is giving me trouble." She pushed back the terrycloth headband on her forehead. "My husband is out of town on a fishing trip, so I can't call him. I noticed your truck. Do you mind taking a look?"

"I don't mind at all." Sidney stood from the bench and

tossed the last bite of his biscuit into the nearby trash can. "Come on, Tater Tot. Let's go work on this nice lady's car."

Hazie May grabbed her biscuit and followed along behind Sidney as the woman continued to talk about her cholesterol and new exercise plan. Sidney nodded when needed, but the woman didn't need any encouragement to fill his ears with her troubles.

The woman opened the door and popped the car's hood. Sidney looked underneath, then stood back up and rubbed his jaw. "Let me grab my toolbox from my truck, and I'll have you back on the road in no time."

"Thank heavens." The woman smiled at Sidney, her face lighting up. "I sure wasn't looking forward to calling Bill and telling him he needed to come home and see about my car."

Sidney retrieved his toolbox and returned to the car with the raised hood. He tightened a few things and fiddled with some others. "You have a lot of buildup on your battery cables," he said, fifteen minutes later. "I'll jump you off and you should be good to go. If it does this again, come to my garage. I will replace your battery and really check everything over." He hopped in his truck, pulled it around in front of the Toyota, and connected the jumper cables. The car cranked right up. "There you go," he said, removing the cables from her car and closing the hood.

"Thank you so much." The woman grabbed his arm and smiled. "How much do I owe you?"

"Not a thing. Happy to do it." The woman climbed into the car, pulling her cell phone out and dialing as she drove away. "Well, that didn't take too long." Sidney looked over to where Hazie May was waiting in the grass near the parking lot. "Hazie May?" She was there the last time he checked. How long ago was that?

The muscles in Sidney's neck and jaw clenched. His eyes scanned the park for a red checked jumper. He turned the engine off and slammed the truck door. *She's got to be nearby. Her little legs couldn't have taken her far. But somebody could have gotten her. Surely not, not in Carson's Bayou. Adelyn was running from her ex. Oh Lord, help me. What have I done?* He cupped his hands around his mouth. "Hazie May." He jogged toward the playground equipment, his voice echoing across the green field. A queasy feeling crept into his gut, and he jumped as his cell phone vibrated in his back pocket. Slowing down near the slide, he pulled out his phone. She was nowhere to be seen. He looked down at the text from Adelyn. Almost back. Will be there in about thirty minutes.

Sidney slowly turned in a circle, his eyes scanning the entire park. The duck pond came into view on the other side of the greenery and he stopped. The pounding in his chest reverberated in his ears, and a vision of Hazie May going under the water flashed into his head. "Dear Lord. Please. Please." He took off in a full run across the park. Why, why had he gotten involved with this woman and her child? Why on earth had he agreed to babysit her today? He wasn't her parent. He barely knew Adelyn. Why had she agreed to leave Hazie May with him anyway?

Sidney finally reached the edge of the pond and sank to his knees. *Thank you, Lord.* His legs wobbled, but he stood, relief washing over him like a wave. Hazie May sat under a nearby oak tree, petting a stray dog. He ran both hands through his hair, blinking as the girl giggled and rolled around in the grass with the animal, completely carefree. His palms pressed against his cheeks, and he sucked in a deep breath of air, regaining his composure.

This had been a huge mistake. All of this. What would have happened if Hazie May had drowned in the pond? Oh, I'm so sorry Adelyn. I was being a Good Samaritan again and accidentally let your daughter die on my watch. Thank goodness they would be gone soon, probably by Monday.

He had almost forgotten why he never got involved in other people's problems. This could have been bad, very bad.

Sidney walked over to the tree and sat in the grass by Hazie May. "You wandered off without telling me where you were going, young lady."

"No, I didn't." Hazie May scooted over and snuggled under Sidney's arm. The dog followed and flopped down on her lap. "I yelled at you when I got to the slide." She stroked the top of the dog's head and turned her eyes up to Sid. "You must not have heard me."

"You asked after you were already way over at the slide?" He looked down; one eyebrow arched. "Do you think that was the correct way to ask permission from the adult who is taking care of you?"

"Prolly not, but you were busy with that lady." Hazie May's chin quivered. "You're not mad, are you, Sid? I didn't mean to do something bad."

"No." Sidney swallowed the lump in his throat, suddenly tired. Exhausted. He hugged Hazie May up closer and ran his hand across the top of her hair. "No. I'm not mad, don't worry. I thought I had lost you there for a minute, and it scared me."

"I'm sorry, Sid. I saw the dog. He wanted a bite of my biscuit. I kind of forgot about you and the lady." She looked up and smiled. "He's a nice dog. He likes biscuits and jam."

"He seems to like you pretty well, too." Sidney looked at the dog hair clinging to Hazie May's clothes. "Come on. Your momma just texted and said she was almost back. She can tell you all about your pawpaw and mawmaw."

"And their swimming pool." Hazie May shoved the dog off her lap and stood up. "I guess we gotta tell him bye, huh?"

"I'm afraid so. He probably belongs to some kid, and they are wondering where he's at." Sidney looked out across the pond before turning back to the parking area on the other side of the park. "Hazie May, can you swim?"

"Not yet. Momma said I have to take lessons soon though. Can you swim?"

"Quack quack." Sidney scooped the giggling child up and placed her on his shoulders. "Call me Quackers. I can out swim any duck around."

"Maybe you can teach me one day."

CHAPTER EIGHT

*a*delyn flipped down the truck visor and looked at her eyes. They were a little red. Hazie May might not see her eyes, but Sidney probably would. Sidney seemed to be pretty good about minding his own business though. If she didn't mention it, there was a good chance he would leave it alone. She killed the engine and climbed out of the truck. Someone rolled the garage door up, so the two had to be around somewhere.

Giggles floated from the back of the garage, and Adelyn stepped into the doorway. She blinked several times, her eyes adjusting to the dimmer lighting. "I'm back," she called, forcing a cheerful tone into her voice. "Did anybody miss me?"

"Momma." Hazie May's chubby legs appeared from around a truck that Sidney had pulled in the night before. "I missed you, but I had a great time with Sid. He took me to the park for breakfast."

"The park?" Adelyn looked from her daughter to Sidney, walking up behind her. "I thought you had to work today."

"I do, but since I'm halfway caught up, I figured I would open after lunch." Sidney smiled and rubbed the top of Hazie May's head. "Since you called saying you were almost back; we came on back too."

"Momma, I saw a dog." Hazie May tugged on the hem of Adelyn's tee-shirt. "Sid said I couldn't keep him though."

"Mr. Sidney was right." *I've got to find a home for me and you. We can't add a dog to my list of things to feed.* "Did you have a good time at the park?"

"I did." Hazie May bobbed her head up and down. "A lady broke her car, and Sid helped her fix it, then he came and found me. I wasn't really lost, Momma." She looked from her mother back to Sidney. "Was I Sid? You didn't even get mad at me or anything?"

"Lost?" Adelyn's eyebrows drew together, and she reached down and picked up Hazie May. She looked at Sidney. "What's she talking about?"

"Well." Sidney cleared his throat and looked past Adelyn to the truck in the parking area. "I, uh."

"Spit it out, Sidney." Adelyn stared at the man until his gaze finally returned to her. "What's she talking about?"

"Momma." Hazie May put hands on either side of Adelyn's face and turned it to her. "I wasn't really lost, remember?"

"Hush, honey." Adelyn pulled her face away from Hazie May's, keeping her voice calm. "Here." She sat her back down and pulled the Snicker bar from her purse. "I got you this at the store. Go play for a second, and let me talk to Mr. Sid."

"Alright." Hazie May started tearing open the wrapper with her teeth. "Sid got this game called Operation from his house, and it's so funny. We were playing it." She touched Adelyn's hand. "Can you play it with me in a minute?"

"Sure, honey. As soon as I'm through talking to Mr. Sidney." Adelyn smiled down at Hazie May's big green eyes.

"Now scoot." Hazie May skipped across the concrete floor to the backside of the garage and plopped down by the ancient-looking board game. Adelyn turned her eyes back to Sidney, staring at her, his lips pressed into a thin line.

"An old lady needed her car jumped off. Hazie May was standing nearby in the grass." Sidney cleared his throat again. "I only took my eyes off her for a minute, and when I looked over, she was gone."

"Gone. What do you mean, gone?"

"I mean." Sidney pulled in a deep breath. "I mean, I looked around and didn't see her. It was only for a minute. I found her with the dog down at the duck pond."

"Duck pond!" Adelyn lowered her voice. "You lost her, and she was near a pond when you found her?" Adelyn heard the anger in her voice. Some of the anger was toward Sidney for letting Hazie May wander away, but a lot of the anger was against herself. It didn't matter. It was rising like a wave and spilling out, overtaking her. "I thought you said you would take care of her for me, Sidney. That means you were supposed to keep your eyes on her and not let her get in harm's way." She spat the words out like bullets, and from the look on Sidney's face they were hitting their target perfectly, wounding with precision. "She could have drowned. Or, or, or what if someone would have grabbed her?" Tears moistened Adelyn's eyes, and her voice grew thick. "She's all I have." She turned her eyes toward the ground and pushed her fingers to her forehead. Sidney stood quietly, and she raised her eyes. "What were you thinking?"

"I'm sorry." Sidney's voice was low, the words heavy, regret weighing them down. "I know you're mad. I would be too if I were you. Um." He glanced again toward his truck, then looked at Adelyn. "I know you are getting ready to leave in a day or two. I'll just try to stay out of your way until you're gone."

Sidney walked away from her to his truck, his shoulders slumped and head down. Tears made their way down Adelyn's cheeks as he climbed in the truck and pulled into the street. He didn't fight back. He didn't deny the accusations. She had never argued with anyone like that before. Zane always had an explanation for everything, getting louder and louder until she pretended to agree with him. Mother always shouted and slammed things around. Sidney took complete responsibility for his actions. No denying or haggling or anything. What was she supposed to do with that? She wiped her eyes with the back of her hand and stared at his truck pulling out of sight. What now? She closed her eyes and opened them slowly, trying to wrap her head around everything that had happened since she got out of bed this morning. He would be back. He had to come back. This was his place, after all.

"Is Sid going to get chocolate chip ice cream?" Hazie May asked, walking over.

"Hmmm?" Adelyn looked down.

"Sid asked me what your favorite ice cream is. He said you would want to celebrate getting to move into my pawpaw and mawmaw's house. He is getting ice cream so we can have a party." Hazie May handed the half-eaten Snicker bar to her mother. "I told him chocolate chip is your favorite."

"Oh." Adelyn sniffed and rubbed the end of her nose. "I think he is going to his house for a little while. Come on. Let's go up to the apartment and get that chocolate off your face."

"When can I go see Sid's house?" Hazie May skipped along beside Adelyn, out of the garage, and to the stairs along the side of the building going up to the apartment. "That's where he got the Operation game. I bet he's got some more toys there, and I could find them if we went to his house for a visit."

"Sounds like you want to go meddle through all of Mr. Sidney's stuff." Adelyn took Hazie May's hand as they ascended the stairs. "I doubt we will be going there any time soon."

"Aww. Why not? I'll ask him before I look in his closet. I promise."

"We have a lot to do around here. Besides, you don't go tromping into someone's house. You wait until they invite you. That's using good manners."

"Like Pawpaw and Mawmaw invited you?" Hazie May turned innocent eyes up at her mother.

"Well." Adelyn bit her lower lip and looked across the lot behind the garage with weeds and brown grass. "It's a little different with family, I guess."

"Sid's family, Momma." Hazie May waited on the miniscule balcony while Adelyn unlocked the apartment door. "Besides, I know he wouldn't care."

Adelyn halfway listened to Hazie May rattle on about games Sidney played as a child and things she wanted to try, like Red Rover and Duck Duck Goose. She flipped the light switch, and they stepped inside the studio loft. Two hundred dollars was still hidden away in her duffle bag. Sidney refused any money she tried to give him toward rent and groceries, or even car repairs. Cleaning and cooking and doing the little bit of work in his office were not nearly enough to repay everything he was doing for her.

Hazie May skipped across the room and disappeared through the bathroom door. Their two duffle bags lay on the floor in the corner. Everything they owned. She had nowhere to go, an ex-husband breathing down her throat waiting for her to make a mistake so he could take her daughter, the only parent who had ever really loved her had died, and she had alienated the only person in the world who had truly been kind to her.

"Momma, can we color?"

"Not right now, honey." Adelyn ran her fingers through her hair and touched the scab on her forehead. "Slip off your shoes." Exhaustion suddenly hit her like a brick wall. "We are going to take a nap."

"But I'm not sleepy." Hazie May's lips poked out like a duck's bill. "I wish I could have gone with Sidney."

"Shoes. Off. Now." Adelyn sat on the bed with the antique spindle frame. Hazie May climbed up beside her as the bedsprings squeaked. The sound was somehow comforting. She slipped her loafers off and helped Hazie May tug off her cowboy boots. "You smell kind of like a dog."

"I washed my face and hands." Adelyn turned her face up and stuck her hands out for inspection. "I can take a bath while you take a nap if you want me to."

"No." Adelyn's lips turned up slightly at the corners as they lay down beside each other. "Let's lay down for just a few minutes and rest. I'll run you a bubble bath after our nap so you will stop smelling like Rover."

"His name's not Rover. I didn't name him, but I'm sure his name's not Rover."

"Close your eyes, Hazie May." Adelyn listened to the child's breathing beside her, slowing as her body relaxed. She closed her eyes and pushed away the image of her mother telling her that her father had died last year. Tears eased out of her eyes and ran down her cheeks. She let them flow, not trying to stop them. She had learned to do her crying at night or nap time when her little girl was asleep. Hazie May was carrying some of this burden, and Adelyn hated herself for it. The child was just so smart. Adelyn didn't tell her things, but she figured things out—sometimes quicker than Adelyn did.

Adelyn's mind slowed down and sleep started to sneak in

around the edges of the worry clouding her thoughts. A rumble of a truck pushed into her dream, and she faded away into emotional exhaustion. Sidney was back. The tension in her neck relaxed. He would listen to her. She didn't know what she was going to tell him or ask him, but he would listen. He would understand.

CHAPTER NINE

Adelyn had every right to be mad. He lost her kid. Sidney unwrapped his beef jerky stick and tore off a bite. He would hang back, stay out of her way until she left to go to her parents. Their leaving was all for the best anyway. Nearly losing Hazie May, that was not for the best. Goose flesh popped up on his forearms. This morning could have turned out bad, very bad. No, thank the Lord everything worked out okay, but it drove home one fact. He was not cut out to be a father, a husband, or even a boyfriend. This situation was different from the girls Fiona kept trying to fix him up with. Those women were single, either working and independent, or with family around them to help them out with any minor problems that came their way. Not Adelyn. She was starting over because of that good-for-nothing bully husband of hers. She also had a child to take care of. The last thing she needed was a man who added worries to her already full plate of concerns.

Sidney sat down in the old lawn chair and adjusted his hips. If he sat in the wrong place, his behind would slip too far into the hole in the woven bottom. When Callie was twelve, she tried to sneak a smoke and dropped the cigarette on the chair, burning a hole through the seat. Nana had whipped her rear end until she thought it was on fire, ending her smoking days forever. Why did he hang on to this broken chair?

His eyes wandered across the overgrown front yard. He still needed to mow. He didn't mind mowing, but for the past couple of weeks he had stayed at the garage until late into the night working on her car. That would be over this weekend, and he would get the yard in shape next week, before Fiona had a conniption fit.

Of course, when Adelyn and Hazie May left, he would move into the apartment. He picked up the can of Coke sitting on the saggy porch floorboards and took a long drink. Yeah, he was getting attached to Adelyn, and that was not good. The buzzing cell phone brought him out of his musings, and he pulled it out of his pocket. One of his customers, the Mustang owner, was coming to the garage in thirty minutes to pick up his car.

Sidney took the last swallow of Coke and crushed the can in his hand. He would stay downstairs and finish up her car this afternoon. Adelyn was furious when he drove off earlier. She would surely stay upstairs, away from him. He stood from the lawn chair, folded it back up, and propped it against the wall. She needed to cool off, and it looked like it was going to take her a while. He would give her the rest of the day, but tomorrow he would apologize again. Even though she was moving out of his life, he didn't want them to part on bad terms. He looked around the living room and kitchen for his truck keys. Her face, tears sparkling from her eyes, flashed through his mind. No, he didn't want to part like that. They had become friends, and friends forgave each other. But losing her child—that was not something one friend would do to the other. He swiped the keys from the kitchen counter. Enough sitting around moping. Time to go get some work done.

"*D*ude. She purrs like a kitten."

Sidney grinned at the man picking up the Mustang. "That's a beautiful car, JT. Be sure you don't get carried away coming home from any of your football games and end up in a ditch. It has a lot of power under the hood."

"I won't, man. I'm working too hard to get the thing paid for to do that." JT turned off the engine and stood from the seat of the car. "My little brother is having an awesome year as quarterback. He told me he has Music Appreciation with your little sister."

"Really?" Sidney wrinkled his brow. He and JT had gone to school together, but never really ran in the same circles. JT, like his little brother, was a one hundred percent football jock. He had gone to the local junior college on a scholarship, then on to the University of Louisiana on another scholarship, and gotten a degree in business. Now he managed a distribution warehouse in a neighboring town. He lived on the other side of Carson's Bayou, but if you wanted to find him any Friday night, go to wherever the local college was playing football. He would be there. "Callie hasn't mentioned that."

"You've got company." JT tilted his head toward the door on the side of the garage. "Your girlfriend?" JT looked back at Sidney. "If she is, you are one lucky man."

"No. She's a friend." Sidney looked behind him where Adelyn stood in the doorway, not particularly caring for the way JT was watching her.

"Well, in that case, do you mind introducing me?" JT ran his hand through the top of his short blond hair and flashed a pearly white grin in Adelyn's direction. "She must not be from around here. I believe I would remember her."

"Maybe another time." Sidney crossed his muscular arms across his chest. "I need to get to work on the next car right now."

"Oh. Well." JT drug his eyes from Adelyn and frowned at Sidney. "Alright. I guess I better be going then." He sat back behind the wheel of the Mustang and cranked the vehicle, revving the motor. "Thanks again, Sidney. Bring your friend to one of Dawson's games. I sure would like to meet her."

Yeah, I bet you would. Sidney watched JT back out of the garage and listened as he floored the gas pedal, roaring the car down the street away from town. Some boys never grew up. He turned and looked at Adelyn leaning against the door frame, biting her lower lip. Should he try to talk to her? No, he needed to stick to his plan, keep his distance. He turned away and walked over to her car.

"Sidney?" Adelyn walked up behind him, her voice quiet. "Can we talk?"

Sidney pulled his head out from under the hood of her car and turned around. "I figured you wouldn't want to talk to me after what I did this morning." He wiped his hands on a rag laying on the grill of the car. "I thought I would give you some space."

"About that." Adelyn stared down at her hands, then finally looked back up. "It could have happened to anybody. I've told Hazie May a thousand times to not walk off, but when she sees a dog or a cat, she forgets everything else." Adelyn rubbed her hands together in front of her. "I'm uh, I think I over-reacted because of what happened with my mother. I'm sorry."

"I'm glad you aren't mad at me." Sidney stared down at

Adelyn. "I figure you will leave in a day or two, and I really didn't want to say goodbye with you being upset with me."

"I'm not mad at you." Adelyn's eyes watered, tears brimming and threatening to run down her face. "You have been so good to me and Hazie May. I know you wouldn't neglect her."

"Adelyn." Sidney reached down and placed his hand on her elbow. "Come on. Let's go sit down in the office for a minute, and you can tell me what's going on. Whatever it is, we will figure something out to make it better."

"Do you mind if we go sit at the top of the stairs? Hazie May is asleep, and I want to be able to hear her if she gets up. She's had so much change in the past couple of weeks. I don't want her to wonder where I am."

"Sure." Sidney walked with Adelyn out the side door and followed her up the steps to the little stoop outside of the apartment door. They sat side by side, and he waited, giving her time to say what was on her mind.

"My father was not there." Adelyn pulled in a deep, ragged breath. "He died last year—and I didn't even know about it." She turned and looked at Sidney, tears now running freely down her cheeks. "I couldn't stay in touch with Father. I couldn't risk Zane finding out about my parents."

Sidney listened to what she was telling him, and his eyebrows pulled together. "Why not? I'm not sure I'm following you."

"Zane . . . I divorced Zane over a year ago, but I figured out right after Hazie May was born that I had to leave him, really, before that. We only dated each other for three months before we married." Adelyn rubbed her fingers under her eyes, wiping away the tears. "It was stupid, but he was so, I don't know, charismatic. He wined and dined me. Treated me like I was the center of his universe. I fell completely and totally under his spell."

"But he changed." Sidney's voice grew deep. "Did he hurt you?"

"He hit me a few times. That's when I took Hazie May and filed for divorce. I stayed with a girlfriend until after everything was final. "But deep down, even from the beginning, something wasn't right. He gave me an allowance, and I had to tell him exactly where I spent every penny. He checked my phone every evening to see who I had called. He wanted to control everything about me. I wasn't a very social person, and I had never really been in a relationship with a man before. When he asked about my parents, I lied and told him they were killed in a car wreck." Adelyn bit down on her lip and stared across the parking lot. "I was still mad at them when we got married and didn't want my mother at my wedding. I was so stupid." She pushed her lips up into a sad smile. "You know what is so crazy?"

"What's that?" Sidney watched Adelyn lean back against the steps, wanting to put his arm around her and make her feel safe, but didn't dare. She wasn't his to protect.

"I lied about my parents being killed in a car wreck, and then that's how my father died." She turned and searched Sidney's face. "Do you think God was punishing me for cutting my parents out of my life? Now my father will never meet Hazie May."

"Look." Sidney shifted his body on the stoop to face Adelyn. "I'm not a Bible scholar, but I know at least one thing. God is good, and He loves His children. Would you punish Hazie May for trying to protect herself from someone who was threatening her?"

"Of course not." Adelyn rubbed the back of her hand across her nose and sniffed.

"Then why do you think God, your heavenly Father, would punish you for trying to protect yourself from this guy, Zane? He knew your heart and saw the trouble you were in."

"You're right." Adelyn nodded. "I shouldn't have lied, but God wouldn't take my father's life because I lied."

"No, He wouldn't. God loves you and wants what's best for you, even when you mess up."

"I've definitely messed up." Adelyn put her hands on her cheeks and looked up at the afternoon sky. White clouds drifted in front of the sun, throwing a shade over them. "I've definitely messed up, and I don't know how to fix it."

"Your car will be done by this evening." Sidney rubbed his hand across his jawline. "You will have your wheels back, and once you get set up in your mother's house, I'm sure you'll be able to find a job and get settled there."

"No. I'm not moving in with my mother." Adelyn pushed her elbows off of the stoop behind her and sat back up, staring across the parking lot. She turned back to Sidney. "I can't go there without my father. I know Mother wouldn't allow it, plus, I don't want Mother to have any kind of influence over Hazie May."

"Oh." A tiny flame flickered in Sidney's heart, but he immediately squashed it out. "So, you will be staying?"

"If you will let me." Adelyn looked at Sidney. "I don't have anywhere else to go."

CHAPTER TEN

The skinny gray kitten's back arched, and its hair stood on end. Sidney watched Adelyn set a saucer of milk on the ground a few feet from the frightened animal. She held Hazie May's hand, and they took a step backwards, giving the kitten some space.

He looked down at the top of his hand where the grey and white kitten scratched him yesterday. "I'm not sure you'll ever tame that thing," he said, eyes narrowed. The kitten eyed them all, hissing and spitting. "It's a mean little beast."

"It's scared." Adelyn sat down next to the back of the garage and leaned against the wall. "That's why the poor thing is acting that way." She pulled Hazie May down into her lap, and they waited. The kitten slowly crept up to the dish and stuck its nose in. It jerked back and snorted, but licked the milk off its face and returned to try again. "Even if we don't tame it enough to pet, maybe we can get it to trust us enough to let us feed it."

"I want to pet it, Momma," Hazie May said, turning to look at her mother. "I think I could catch it while it's drinking the milk."

"You probably could," Adelyn said, running her fingers through the child's wild morning curls. "But then it would get scared again and scratch you the way it did Mr. Sidney. You have to let it relax; it has to learn to trust us enough so it will come to us."

A car horn tooted around the front of the building, and Sidney looked at his watch. 7:45. He didn't open until 8:00. He arrived at the apartment at 7:00 for breakfast as usual. After they finished the pancakes and bacon, Hazie May saw the kitten out the window at the back of the apartment. He heard it crying yesterday in the tall grass as he was leaving for the evening. After backing the thing into a corner, he had grabbed it and brought it back to the garage. That's when he got the scratch. It must have escaped into the yard again during the night.

"I better get around front and raise the doors." Sidney pushed off the wall where he was leaning and looked down at Adelyn. "Looks like it's going to be a busy day."

"I'll get Hazie May dressed, and we will be out to mind the office in a bit." Adelyn smiled up at Sidney.

"No rush." Sidney walked around to the front of the garage, the morning sun shining into his eyes. A black SUV without a speck of dust anywhere on it set in the parking area, the windows tinted too dark to see the driver. He went in the side entrance, flipped on the lights, and rolled up the garage door. Hazie May had taped a drawing of a little girl and a dog to the side of one of the toolboxes. Sidney smiled. It had been two weeks since Adelyn asked if she could stay and things were going well. The steady stream of vehicles coming in for mechanic and body work was keeping him busy, extremely busy. He ate his meals with Adelyn, and she worked in the office, but there had not been any time for them to sit and talk or spend any time together. Breakfast was a hurried affair; lunch was usually a bologna sandwich or something similar eaten while he continued to work. By the time he was ready for dinner, Adelyn would bring a plate down for him. She and Hazie May had already eaten their meal.

Even though something inside him longed to make time to just be with Adelyn, to go for a walk, or sit and listen to the radio and chat, the practical side, the side that mattered, reminded him he was lucky she was his friend. When she asked him to go with them to the park this past Saturday, he said he was too busy. On Sunday, when she texted to see what time he would pick them up for church, he asked her to go in her own car since he was running late. This morning at breakfast, Adelyn continued to be polite, but the warmth she showed before had cooled. He ran his finger over Hazie May's drawing and a lump of regret rose in his throat. He pushed it down and turned back toward the garage doors. No, he was doing the right thing, for him and for Adelyn.

"Do you own the red truck parked over there?"

Sidney looked at the thin woman in the gray pant suit, silver hair pulled back away from her serious face. "Yes, ma'am, I do. I'm Sidney Madison and this is my business." He looked closer at the woman's face. She seemed a little familiar, but where had he met her?

"My name is Deborah Swan." The woman looked around the garage, then turned her eyes back to Sidney. "My daughter came to see me a couple of weeks ago driving that red truck. How do you know her?"

That's why she looked familiar. She resembled Adelyn around the eyes, but where Adelyn's eyes were soft, warm, this woman's were hard, judgmental. "Your daughter works for me." Sidney didn't say anything else. According to what Adelyn told him, Deborah Swan was not someone she wanted to share her business with. He wasn't good at a lot of things, but keeping tight lips was something he did well.

Deborah Swan tilted her chin down, waiting for Sidney to tell her more. "Well?" she finally asked, glaring down her nose. "Is she here?"

"She hasn't gotten to work yet." Sidney met the woman's stare. "Do you want me to give her a message?"

"Yes. Tell her to call me. We need to talk." The woman pulled a card from her purse and handed it to Sidney. "I saw a coffee shop on the other side of town. Tell her I will be in town for a couple of hours and I need to speak to her in person."

Sidney took the glossy card and nodded. The woman walked out of the garage and got back in her SUV. He looked down at the card. Deborah Swan, Attorney at Law. Adelyn's mother was a lawyer? She definitely looked the part. He slipped the card into his pocket. He would give it to Adelyn when she came down. What she did after that was her business.

*A*delyn pulled into a parking space across the street from the Bayou Bean. She had never visited the coffee shop before, but heard the people at church talk about it. The fancy looking restaurant across the street where she parked apparently used to be a homeless shelter run by the local churches.

She grabbed her purse off the passenger's seat and got out of her car. Her mind darted in several directions as she jogged across the busy street. She couldn't keep mooching off Sidney forever. A temporary stay at a homeless shelter might be in her and Hazie May's future if she didn't get on the ball and find an actual job.

Adelyn stepped onto the sidewalk and hurried into the Bayou Bean. She looked around the cheery coffee house and breathed in deeply. The aroma of freshly ground coffee and yeasty pastries tickled her nose. She had dropped Hazie May off at Fiona's house, or mansion really, while she came to meet her mother. Maybe she would get Fiona a pastry as a thank you for babysitting her daughter on such short notice.

Deborah Swan sat in the corner looking down at her phone. Adelyn shifted the strap of her bag on her shoulder and bit her lower lip. Why was her mother here? There was a motive. That was certain, and whatever it was, it was something her mother would profit from, either in status or finances. Her mother scrolled through her phone, cool and in control, and a burning ache started in Adelyn's gut.

She could just turn around and go back to the garage. No, for the past couple of days, Sidney had started acting strange. It looked like she was wearing out her welcome with him and would have to move on soon. He hadn't been rude, or given her any ultimatums. Honestly, she couldn't imagine him doing that. He was too nice of a guy. He was just distant, more quiet and reserved. She took a step toward her mother's table, ignoring the sensation in her gut. If she didn't confront her and get this over with today, Mother would keep coming back. A pit bull with a pork chop didn't have anything on Deborah Swan when it came to hanging on to something she wanted.

"Hello, Mother." Adelyn pulled the wooden chair out across from Mrs. Swan and sat down. "How did you find me?"

"The license plate. A friend at the courthouse tracked it down." Mrs. Swan took a sip of her coffee and sat it back on the table. Her French tip manicured fingers drummed against the Styrofoam cup. "I have a proposition for you."

Mrs. Swan looked across the table at Adelyn, waiting for a response. Her brow didn't wrinkle, but Adelyn figured the expertly injected Botox prevented any of that. People had thought Mother was her sister for years, and Deborah Swan lapped it up like biscuits and red-eye gravy. "What kind of proposition?"

"I have a couple of little rental houses back in Lakeside. One is empty right now. You can move in, and I won't charge you rent until you get settled in and find a job." Mother picked up the coffee cup but set it back down without taking another sip. "I've talked to Jerry Roberts, the Circuit Court Judge. He said he will get you a job at the courthouse."

Adelyn eyed her mother. She had given Sidney her business card earlier, saying she was a lawyer, and technically, she was. She graduated, passed the bar, but as soon as she married Father, she quit her job and never worked another day. She still kept those cards and gave them to people she either wanted to impress or intimidate. "Why are you doing this, Mother? What's in it for you?"

"You are my daughter. The only relative I have left in the world." Mrs. Swan tilted her chin up and looked down her nose. "We need to put the past behind us and act like adults. Once you get a few paychecks, you can pay the rent and have a decent home. You won't have to visit me or have anything to do with me if you don't want to. I'll know you are taken care of." Her eyes narrowed, and she stared at Adelyn. "What are you doing at that grease-monkey's shop, anyway? That's not a respectable place for a woman to be working. I was afraid you got yourself into something like this. I told your father you would eventually come crawling back, but he never believed me. I wish he was here to see that I was right."

"Yeah." Adelyn looked across the table, voice monotone. "Yeah, I imagine you do." She pulled in a deep breath and blew it out through her nose. "Look, Mother. I don't know what you are up to, but what you need to do is forget I ever came by. I am not moving into one of your houses. Go back to Lakeside and play tennis with your girlfriends and do all the things that seem to make you happy. I'm fine where I'm at."

"You're hiding something." Mrs. Swan frowned at her daughter. "I could always tell when you were in trouble. I'll go back home, but when whatever it is you are running from catches up with you, come find me. I may help you because you are my flesh and blood, but only if it won't bring scandal on my name."

Adelyn got up from the table and headed out the door, not looking back at her mother. She would not go home now. It was a good thing her mother found her. The reality of who her mother was had dimmed a little over the past five years. No, she would never get back under her mother's control. She would move into that shelter here in Carson's Bayou before she let that happen. Why was Mother offering her help? Something was up. She unlocked her car and slid behind the wheel. It didn't matter. Whatever her mother was scheming, she would not be a part of.

CHAPTER ELEVEN

Sidney walked to the mouth of the garage and leaned against the opening. Fiona lifted Hazie May from the Tahoe seat to the ground. Adelyn had left that morning with Hazie May not long after he gave her the business card and the note from her mother. He wanted to tag along, and her refusal put a knot in his stomach. In the end, he returned to work, and she left without him. She must have gotten Fiona to take care of Hazie May. Good. The two women were becoming friends, and Adelyn needed someone dependable in her life.

"We got pizza," Hazie May said, walking up to Sidney and holding her arms open for a hug. "Fiona has the biggest dog I've ever seen in my life."

Sidney squatted down and hugged the child. He would miss her chatter, her hugs, her laughter when they moved away. He smiled as she scurried around to the back of the building in search of the kitten. "Stay near the garage, Hazie May," he called after her. He turned to Fiona, walking up beside him. "Hey, Sis." The two continued around the back of the garage. The child was peering at the kitten from a safe distance. "How did you end up with Hazie May?"

"I told Adelyn Sunday that if she ever needed a babysitter to give me a call." Fiona propped against the edge of the garage. "She called this morning, and I told her I'd love to keep Hazie May while she met with her mother and ran some errands." Fiona cut her eyes toward her brother. "She said she thought she was wearing her welcome out with you and didn't want to ask you to babysit the child."

"No." Sidney's eyes stretched wide, staring at his sister. "I don't mind helping out at all. I just . . ." Sidney looked over at Hazie May as she followed the kitten into the field of tall grass. "Come back this way, Hazie May. Snakes like to hide out in those weeds." Hazie May poked out her bottom lip but stepped back toward the mowed section of the yard. Sidney turned to Fiona. "I watched her for Adelyn a couple of weeks ago. I took her to the park, and I lost her."

"Lost her?" Fiona's eyebrows shot up. "Well, you obviously found her again. Was she okay?"

"She was fine. We probably weren't apart for no more than ten minutes, fifteen at the most." Sidney reached down and pulled a dandelion from the grass at his feet. "In that few minutes, though, I almost lost my mind." He twirled the flower between his finger and the fuzzy white petals turned loose from the stem and floated through the air. "I decided it's probably better for all of us if I keep to myself where they are concerned. I mean, who loses a child?"

"Big brother." Fiona reached over and put her hand on Sidney's shoulder. "I don't know what we are going to do with you. I would have lost Hazie May earlier out at the house when she played with Lester if there hadn't been a fence around the yard. Those things happen, and nothing bad came of it." She tilted her head forward and searched Sidney's down-turned face. "Was Adelyn mad?"

"She was at first, but we talked about it, and then she was fine."

"Then what's your problem? Adelyn really likes you, Sid, and more than that, I think she needs you, too."

"I'm helping her." Sidney kept his eyes on the child walking along the edge of the tall grass, ignoring Fiona's scrutiny. Hazie May cooed and talked to the kitten, coaxing it into the safety of the mowed yard. "I'll keep helping her, but I can't let myself get close to her." He dropped the flower stem on the ground and turned to Fiona. "What if I'm like our father? You don't remember him, but I do. He was not a good guy."

"What if I'm like our mother?" Fiona asked, rolling her eyes. "I'm pregnant, Sid. What if I decide in a couple of years to just up and leave my child because of some strange Madison trait handed down from our mother to me? Can't you see how ridiculous that sounds?" She bit her lower lip, staring at her brother. "God brought these people into your life. Have you prayed about this decision to snub Adelyn, Sidney? I can't see the Lord guiding you to make the woman feel unwanted."

"No. No, I haven't. I wouldn't call it snubbing her anyway." Sidney rubbed his hand along the back of his neck. "I've already messed up once. I didn't want to take a chance on it happening again and really hurting them. Adelyn doesn't deserve that."

"Things happen." Fiona leaned her head onto her brother's arm. "You have to quit worrying about mistakes you might make and put yourself out there. I can tell you one thing for sure, though, you are hurting Adelyn already by pulling away from her."

"What did she say?" Sidney asked, a frown creeping over his face.

"She didn't say anything in particular, but I could see it on her face when she talked about the way you've been acting for the past several days."

"I'm not trying to hurt her."

"I know that, Sid. You're a good guy. You are not our father any more than I'm our mother. For one thing, they didn't know the Lord, and we do. Pray about this. The Bible says it's not good for a man to be alone." Fiona looked over to Hazie May squatting down at the edge of the tall grass. The little gray kitten was easing up to her and sniffing her hand. "You are just like that stray cat. You are backing away because you are scared, but if you can't trust yourself . . . trust God.

Talking to her mother had turned out to be a good thing. Adelyn took a bite of the Butterfinger and waited for the red light to turn green. She had played the part of the victim long enough, and this morning's conversation was the kick in the pants she needed to change that.

She had called Fiona after leaving the lawyer's office to tell her she was on her way to pick Hazie May up, and she said they were back at Sidney's garage. She hurried through town, eager to tell Sidney about her plan. Maybe, if he saw she was making an effort to get things straightened out and get on her feet, he would go back to the old Sidney. She needed friends like Sidney, and Fiona too, and didn't want their friendship to be all about them giving her handouts.

Adelyn pulled her car into the gravel parking area in front of the shop and smiled. Old McDonald was playing on the radio coming from the garage instead of the usual country music Sidney played. He really was a good guy. "Anybody home?" she called, stepping into the doorway.

"Nobody here but us chickens," Fiona said, coming out of

the office. Hazie May followed behind her with the gray kitten in her arms.

"Look, Momma." Hazie May hurried over to Adelyn, her face beaming. "He finally likes me. I named him Peter."

"Peter? I like that name." Adelyn looked down at the scrawny kitten now purring contentedly in her daughter's arms. "Honey, you can feed the poor thing and pet it, but you shouldn't bring it inside. Mr. Sidney might not want a cat in here." Sidney slid out from under a truck on the other side of the garage and walked over to where they were.

"He said I could bring it in." Hazie May's jaw grew firm. "He said he would take me to the dollar store to get it a collar and some food, too."

"That is, if you don't care," Sidney said, looking at Adelyn, a tentative smile on his lips.

"No, that's fine, if you're sure you don't mind."

"See, Momma?" Hazie May smiled triumphantly at Adelyn. She turned and looked at Fiona. "I'm going to go let Peter finish the bowl of milk. Will you come with me?"

Fiona smiled down at Hazie May, then looked up at Sidney. "I sure will." She looked Sidney in the eye, then turned away. "Let's go see if we can find something for Peter to play with."

"How did things go with your mother?" Sidney asked, watching Fiona and Hazie May walk away.

"The meeting with Mother didn't surprise me. She was nicer than usual, which means she's up to something, but I don't know what." Adelyn waited as Fiona shut the office door and turned back to Sidney. "I'm sorry you are being dragged into all of this. I wanted to tell you though that I went to see a lawyer after my visit with Mother. I'm going to try to get the ball rolling to force Zane to pay the child support he owes. I'm also going to see about trying to get a job and a place to stay. If we are going to be here in Carson's

Bayou, I need to start making some changes to get on my feet."

"Look." Sidney glanced down at his worn work boots, then up at Adelyn. "I need to apologize for the impression I gave you."

"No, you don't," Adelyn said, cutting him off. "I understand you were only expecting to have us here for a few days."

"Listen," Sidney said, slowly raking his hand across his jawline. "It's not that I don't want you here. That's not it at all. Honestly, I really enjoy having you around. The thing is." He paused and pulled in a deep breath. "You had me look after your child, and I almost lost her. I'm not sure I am the kind of guy you can rely on, and the last thing I want to do is cause you more heartache."

"Sidney." Adelyn laid her hand on his forearm. A soft tingle ran up her hand and a slight blush reddened her cheeks. "You have been kinder and more concerned about my welfare than anyone has in—well, in years. You have no idea how much I appreciate you." She pulled her hand away and looked into his eyes. "Knowing that you are my friend means the world to me. I know our friendship has been a little one sided, but if you will give me a chance, I will one day be as good a friend to you as you are to me."

Sidney's lips turned up at the corners. "You already have. I'm, uh." Sidney looked past Adelyn to the truck up on the rack, waiting to be worked on. "I'm better with cars than I am with people. Other than my sisters, I don't talk to many folks. Having you here made me realize how lonely my life is." He turned his eyes back to Adelyn's face. "Your friendship has become a blessing to me."

"I'm sorry I had such a fit the other day about Hazie May and the park," Adelyn said, a tentative smile forming on her lips. "I was already so upset about my father that when you told me what happened, I kind of just blew up." She bit down on her bottom lip. "Can't we forget about that and start over? Go back to how things were?"

"Sure," Sidney nodded. "I'd like that. As a matter of fact. Why don't we go out tonight, the two of us, and grab a bite to eat? You can tell me about the lawyer, and we can talk about your getting a job."

"I'll have to ask Fiona if she can take care of Hazie May again," Adelyn said, the smile growing bigger. "If she can, I would love to."

"I'm sure she can," Sidney said, listening to Fiona's laughter and Hazie May's giggles floating from behind the office door.

CHAPTER TWELVE

*A*delyn rubbed the clear lip gloss across her bottom lip and looked at her reflection in the bathroom mirror. She hadn't worn makeup in weeks. The mascara and lip gloss felt odd on her face. She touched her hand to the waves of hair resting on her shoulder. If she just had the accessories to put it up somehow, but she had not brought anything like that with her in her hurry to leave. If she had not left the cosmetics in the bottom of her purse, she would not have that now either.

The baby blue cotton pull over sweater didn't scream elegance. Neither did the nicest of the three pairs of jeans she had pulled from her duffle bag. They would have to do, though. Besides, she ate dinner with Sidney every evening. They had shared almost every meal since he rescued her from the side of the road. Tonight wasn't any different. Dinner with a friend, nothing more. She tucked her hair behind her ear and glanced at her reflection again. A flutter in her gut made her smile. This afternoon when she had touched Sidney's arm, had he felt that too? That—what was it, tingle? She gently rubbed the faint scar on her hairline. Dinner with a friend. That was all.

Tap, tap, tap. Adelyn tucked a stray wisp of hair back into place and hurried from the bathroom. She slowed her steps, walked across the room, and opened the door.

"I like you in that shirt," Sidney said, smiling down at her. "It really makes your eyes blue. Kind of like those flowers that grow on the fence behind my house. I think Callie calls them morning glories."

Adelyn reached her hand up and touched the edge of her sweater. She breathed in his spicy aftershave and smiled up at Sidney, his damp hair curling at his neck. "Thank you. You look nice yourself," she said, her eyes taking in his green polo, jeans, and cowboy boots. "I wish I had a dress or some slacks or something to wear besides my jeans. I hope I won't be under dressed for where you want to eat."

"No. You look very nice. I thought we could eat at the Gumbo Hut, then go to the park for a walk. How does that sound?"

"Perfect." Adelyn turned and grabbed her purse from the dresser. "We can pick up Hazie May on the way home." Just dinner with a friend.

There were always people at the Gumbo Hut, even on a Monday evening, but it wasn't as crowded as the weekend. Sidney held open the door, and Adelyn entered ahead of him. The teenage waitress placed them at a table near the window on the opposite side of the restaurant from the jukebox. They sat down as a Tim McGraw song filled the air around them.

"What should I get?" Adelyn said, looking at the laminated menu. "The po'boy was good the other day, but I want to try something different."

"I always get the burger." Sidney glanced down at the menu, then laid it back on the table. "I guess one day I'll get burned out on them and try something else, but not yet."

"Hmmm." Adelyn's eyebrows pulled down over her nose. "I haven't had red beans and rice in ages. I think I'll try that." She looked around the room at the few families, men in work clothes, and a couple of groups of teens sitting at the tables. "This is a busy little place for a Monday."

"Everyone says the food is good." Sidney followed her eyes around the room. "Plus, there's not much else to pick from other than the fancy restaurant they put up on the old side of town across from the coffee shop."

"That's where I met Mother this morning, at the coffee shop." Adelyn smiled at the waitress, who appeared and took their orders. "That's a nice area of town," she said as the waitress hurried away to the kitchen.

"It is. It used to be the rundown part of Carson's Bayou, but over the past couple of years, more locally owned businesses opened up there." The song on the jukebox finished, and the soft chatter of the locals took its place. "I hate that you and your mother can't work things out." Sidney looked across the table at Adelyn. "I know what it's like to not be able to depend on a parent."

"My mother has never acted much like a mother. At least not the type of mother my friends seemed to have. If it hadn't been for my father growing up, I don't know how I would have made it." Adelyn paused as the waitress returned with the enormous tumblers full of sweet tea. "I had plenty of material things, and she made sure I was dressed in the best clothes." She watched the waitress move on to another table to take the order from an elderly couple and a little boy. "But Mother was always too busy to be bothered with the real me, and I was not the me she wanted everybody to see. Father came to the school when I broke my arm in second grade, and he always took me to soccer practice and all the other things that Mother never even attempted to be interested in." She pulled the paper from her straw and shoved it in the tea glass. "That's why I knew her sudden interest today in making sure I have a place to live has some kind of ulterior motive."

"Are you sure you want to stay here in Carson's Bayou?" Sidney watched Adelyn sip her tea. "Don't get me wrong. I am glad you are staying, really glad. But my momma and daddy ditched me and my sisters when we were little. If our Nana hadn't taken us in, I don't know what would have happened to us. Family is important." He picked up his straw and slowly tore away the wrapper. "I would hate for you to make a decision now and regret it later."

"No, I'm sure. If you ever get to know my mother, you will understand." Adelyn ran her tongue along her lower lip. "This tea is excellent."

"Yeah. You can buy it by the gallon here. Everybody loves Gumbo Hut tea." Sidney put his straw in his glass and swirled around the crushed ice. "Your mother sounds like my father," he said slowly, looking down at his tea glass. "My last memory of him was when I punched him after he yelled at my mother."

"Oh man, Sidney. That's terrible. How old were you?"

"Just a kid. Five. Even after he yelled at her and told her he didn't want his own kids, my mother still left us with Nana and went with him. I never have understood that."

"Here I am going on and on about my parents, and yours makes mine seem like the Brady Bunch." Adelyn reached across the table and squeezed Sidney's hand. "Was it better at your grandmother's?"

"She was an exceptional woman." Sidney swallowed. The

warmth of Adelyn's hand spread up his arm, across his chest. The heat continued, and he paused, his eyes searching Adelyn's face. "I was blessed to have her," he finally said. "Like Hazie May is to have you."

"I'm glad." Adelyn pulled her hand back across the table and a frown creased her brow. "I'm worried about Hazie May. I need to get her back in preschool and in a steady routine. I have to see about getting her child support going like the judge ordered. I sure hope the lawyer can help me tomorrow. I'm really nervous about seeing him. His name is Carson, Clay Carson. Do you know him?"

"No, afraid not, but Fiona's sister-in-law works at a law office run by a Carson. We can ask her and see if this is the same guy."

"Thank you," Adelyn said. "I know Zane is going to twist things around and make it appear like I'm not being a good parent or something, but I must stand up to him. Hazie May deserves to receive the child support, and there's absolutely no reason for him to not pay it. He's an oral surgeon. He has the money. It's just another way he is forcing his control onto me."

"I have an idea." Sidney looked up as the waitress approached and sat plates in front of them. She asked if they needed anything else, then left them again. The spicy aroma of the sausage floated up in the steam from Adelyn's red beans and rice. "Why don't I go with you tomorrow? I can help you listen to what the lawyer says and be there for moral support, too."

"Are you sure you don't mind? The appointment is at ten in the morning." Adelyn's eyes shined. "I really would appreciate having you there."

"I don't mind at all." Sidney smiled. "Count on me going with you."

"It is so peaceful out here." Adelyn looked across the park toward the pond in the distance. The sun disappeared behind the row of pine trees, and the evening sky glowed pink and purple. A goose honked as a V formation of birds flew across the sky, and crickets sang their bedtime song from somewhere hidden in the grass. A faint chill of fall caressed her skin, and she rubbed her hand down her arm. "I'll have to bring Hazie May back here one evening. She would love to see the sunset and watch the stars come out."

"When I was a kid, there were fireflies everywhere, but you don't see as many nowadays." Sidney looked down at Adelyn hugging her arms to her chest. "I wish I had a coat to give you. Do you mind if I put my arm around your shoulders? You look chilly."

"I am, just a little." Adelyn looked up at Sidney's face through the dim evening light. "No, I don't mind," she said, her voice becoming quiet. "Why don't we go sit on that bench for a while?"

Sidney raised his arm and draped it around Adelyn's shoulders, pulling her closer to his side. They strolled toward the bench, and Adelyn's eyes turned back to the ever-darkening path before them. The heat from Sidney's side warmed her. She closed her eyes and inhaled the scent of his aftershave. She needed to lean on him; she wanted to lean on him, but could she? That flutter in her gut started again, and she forced her eyes open. Lean on him as a friend, of course. That's what she meant, a friend.

They walked up the grassy incline to the bench and sat down, Sidney's arm still around her shoulders. "I am so thankful you are the one who came along the day the deer hit my car," Adelyn said, turning to Sidney, straining her eyes in the darkness. Her breath caught in her chest. His face was so close. His eyes looking down at her. His lips were right there, just out of reach.

"Can I . . ."

Adelyn didn't wait for Sidney to finish the question. She leaned closer, her lips touching his. Their kiss grew and his hand slipped up her shoulder and his palm cradled the back of her head. Adelyn's heart thudded in her chest. Her hand reached up and found Sidney's jaw, slightly rough with a five o'clock shadow.

"Adelyn."

Sidney pulled away. Adelyn slowly opened her eyes, her fingers gliding across his face until he was out of reach, leaving her grasp empty. She looked at his face, but the sunlight was gone, replaced by dim moonlight and shadows. "I'm sorry. I thought you wanted to kiss me."

"I did. I do." Sidney's husky voice cut through the darkness. "I just need to make sure that you understand me." Crickets chirped in the silence. "I'm not sure I'm good at this sort of thing, Adelyn. The boyfriend thing," Sidney finally continued. "I may let you down again."

"I married the perfect man," Adelyn said, searching for Sidney's eyes. The lamppost nearby buzzed, and a soft yellow glow appeared, letting her see the man she was looking for. "I would rather see your flaws, your honest mistakes, the real you, than have you try to make me believe you are this man that deserves to be on a pedestal." She saw the concern in Sidney's eyes and her heart squeezed. "I'm willing to take a chance if you are."

CHAPTER THIRTEEN

*L*ast night had not turned out as expected. He was not upset. No, definitely not upset, just concerned. He had placed his arm around her and pulled her close. The gesture was one of the rightest things he had ever felt in his life, like she was supposed to be there. They sat on the bench, and he had leaned over, intending to whisper in her ear. "Can I hold you like this a little while longer?"

Adelyn; however, leaned in and kissed him. A feeling had surged beyond rightness to something else, something great and warm and exciting . . . something that would have rapidly taken over his being. Even this morning, after a night of rolling and tumbling, his mind and heart were still doing battle. Her thick soft hair in his hand and the pressure of her lips, the warmth of her touch pulled him in making his heart pound of its on accord. Would he enjoy kissing her again? Absolutely, but he was not that guy who jumped into things without thinking them through. It was not good for him. Even more so, and more importantly, it wasn't good for Adelyn.

She was in a vulnerable place. Her world was flipping one

way and then the other, and she needed someone to go along with her for the ride. He could do that. He would do that. He was committed to doing that now. She needed a friend with a sturdy set of shoulders, and he wanted to be that friend, desperately wanted to be that friend. Friendships could lead to something more. This was true. Hopefully it would, some day when Adelyn was in a place to see him clearly for who he was, a garage mechanic who shied away from people and had a broken past. She needed to make sure this was what she wanted.

One day when she had it all together, and she would get it all together, no doubt about that, they would see where they stood. When she was not struggling and just wanting someone to lean on, if she still wanted to pursue their friendship into the beyond, then he would be ready—and she would too. The memory of her lips pushing against his squeezed his heart, but he shoved the need to explore this longing down to that place where he stored everything until he could deal with it slowly, carefully.

Sidney stepped onto the saggy front porch, and a drop of water splattered onto his nose. The roof was leaking. At least it was the porch and not inside. He glanced back at the front door. Maybe it wasn't inside. It wasn't in his bedroom, the bathroom, or kitchen. That was pretty much the only places he used in the place. His bedroom furniture, or what there was of it, was at the apartment being used by Adelyn and Hazie May.

The first night he slept at the house after Adelyn moved into the apartment, he slept in Fiona's room on her bed. That was just weird. Waking up and not seeing his familiar oak tree out the window with the bird feeder he had made in sixth grade VBS seemed odd. Yes, he was a grown man, and no, nobody would know that he was nostalgic about a few things. That evening he had dragged Fiona's twin box spring and mattress to his own room, sleeping there ever since. He left his sister's empty bed frame in her room, like a skeleton from a life that had died away. He hadn't bothered moving a dresser. He had folded his clothes and stacked them either in the clothes basket on the floor in the corner or on the kitchen chair somebody, probably Callie, had brought in there a long time ago. It had never found its way back to the kitchen, and now was missing from where it should be in the apartment.

He should go walk through the house and check for leaks. He turned back to go inside but stopped. His phone vibrated in his back pocket and he pulled it out. A wreck on the highway over near the college happened earlier this morning, before the sun came up. Someone had taken that curve too fast in the rain and hydroplaned into another vehicle coming the other way.

Sidney looked at his phone screen. 7:15. He usually ate breakfast with Adelyn and Hazie May around 7:30, then went downstairs to the shop at 8:00. He had the only wrecker in town. If he didn't go, they would call another place in the next parish like they had to do when he worked at Floyd's garage. That was not good for his business. He pulled in a deep breath and shut the front door a second time. "I'll head that way now," he said to the deputy. The wreck site was only fifteen minutes from the garage. He could swing by, drop off his truck, and get the tow truck. He could get the job done and make it back in plenty of time to go to the lawyer's office with Adelyn. No problem.

Cold rain misted on Sidney's head as he trudged through the wet grass and mud to his truck. It was going to be a nasty day, but at least the rain was slowing some. The temperature had dropped overnight, and the grey cloudy skies and dim sunlight promised that winter was going to come soon, even though fall still felt a lot like summer. He hopped in his truck and started the engine. There's a wreck and they need the tow truck. *I won't be at breakfast, but will be back in plenty of time to go to the lawyer's office with you.* Sidney looked at the text. Heart emoji? No, that was dumb. Plus, he was a friend. He pushed send and tossed his phone over on the truck seat. He had a spare work shirt in the office at the garage. No doubt he would get muddy and greasy picking up the vehicle, but he could change his shirt. The lawyer wouldn't care what he was wearing, anyway. He just didn't want to embarrass Adelyn.

"*I* wish Sid was here." Hazie May stuck her finger in the glob of strawberry jam on her plate and twirled it around. "I wanted to show him the trick Fiona learned me about the church and the steeple and the people."

"Taught me." Adelyn sipped her coffee. "You can show him at lunch. Now quit playing in your breakfast and eat."

"Fiona showed you the trick, too?" Hazie May licked the jam from her finger, letting a small drop dribble down onto her nightgown. "Let's do it together."

"No, you said learned me." Adelyn leaned over and wiped the spot of jam from Hazie May's gown with her thumb. "You should say taught me. That's the correct way to say the sentence." She licked the dab of jam from her thumb and smiled at her daughter's inquisitive face. "I do know the poem though. We can show him at lunch. I bet he knows it, too."

Hazie May turned up her Strawberry Shortcake cup that was probably older than Adelyn and drained the last drop of milk. "Can we go feed Peter now? I'm done."

"Give me just another minute." Adelyn took another sip

from her coffee mug. "Run and find your shoes and get them on while I finish my coffee."

Adelyn watched Hazie May's tangled mess of dark curls slide from the chair and wander over to the other side of the apartment, chanting the little poem. "Here's the church, here's the steeple. Open the doors. Where's the people?"

She listened to the tow truck engine starting in the parking lot below, the sound of the diesel engine distinct from Sidney's other vehicle. *Lord, be with whoever was in that wreck. Keep Sidney safe on the wet roads. Lord, please be with me when I go to the lawyer's office. I want to do right by my daughter, and I know I can't do this alone. Thank you so much for sending Fiona into my life to help. Lord, thank you for Sidney. He really has been a godsend.*

Time to get up and get things done. Drudging through the rain to feed a scrawny grey cat was not high on Adelyn's list of priorities this morning, but it was important to Hazie May. She walked over to the kitchen counter and pulled a couple of empty dollar store bags from under the sink.

"You look funny, Momma," Hazie May said, watching her mother wrap the bag around her head and tie it under her chin. "The bag is sticking up and you have ears like a cat."

"At least my head will be dry. Come here. You are wearing a bag hat." Adelyn squatted down in front of her daughter and tied the bag in place. "Do your feet look funny to you? Kind of like a duck's feet?"

"Yeah." Hazie May sighed, staring down at her pink tennis shoes, the Velcro closures standing straight up. "I got them on the wrong feet."

"Yes, but it's an easy fix." Adelyn scooped up the little girl and sat her on the countertop. "Now, let's get your shoes fixed and find a blanket to throw around us. Poor Peter will think we've forgotten about him if we don't show up with his breakfast."

The wreck site was up the road about a quarter mile. He could see it, but he couldn't get there, not this way anyway. Why hadn't he thought about that, especially near the college. Cars were lining both sides of the highway and traffic was literally moving at a snail's pace, going nowhere for the past thirty minutes. He looked over to the side of the road into the slippery ditch full of rainwater. The tow truck might be able to drive through that if he attempted to go around the long line of cars to where the fire truck and law enforcement vehicles were waiting, but then again, he might get stuck. Then where would he be? He couldn't back up and turn around either. The bumper to bumper traffic had him trapped.

Claude, the deputy who called him earlier, had already jogged down from the crash site in his yellow slicker suit to where Sidney waited. "Take this next right on Blair Road. You have to go around behind the college and cut back through the old side of town, but if you follow the road around, you come out on Cane Road right by the wreck. I know it's a pain, man, but it's the only way to get up to where we are right now. The highway is going to be blocked for at least another couple of hours."

Sidney looked around on the truck seat for his cell phone. The tow truck crept up to the side road as the two vehicles in front of him turned off as the deputy instructed, taking alternate routes to get to wherever they were going. He fished his phone from the floorboard and looked at the time. 8:45. So much for getting back to the garage by ten, much less the lawyer's office. He slammed the palm of his hand against the old steering wheel and watched the truck ahead of him turn onto Blair Road, red brake lights flashing every other second as they crept along, waiting for the bottleneck of traffic to ease.

Stuck in traffic at the wreck site. Not going to make it back in time. I am so sorry. Sidney hit the send button and tossed the cell phone back on the seat. This. This was why he didn't need to get too close to Adelyn. Nana's voice rang in his ears, keeping time with his windshield wipers. "People with good intentions make promises. People with good character keep them."

CHAPTER FOURTEEN

"*T*hank you so much." Adelyn vigorously pumped the arm of the beautiful black-haired woman. "It really is true what they say about small towns and everybody knowing everybody."

"It seems to be that way here in Carson's Bayou," Vivian said, easing her hand from Adelyn's. "I will talk to Lucas this afternoon about your housing situation. You can fill out the application for the next building project, but until then, I am certain he can help you find a place to live."

"I don't know how to thank you." Hope sparkled in Adelyn's eyes. "When I got here, I felt so intimidated, but you are very good at your job, almost like a social worker and a lawyer combined." She adjusted her purse on her shoulder and glanced around the office. "Okay, I guess that's it then. I will go by the elementary school when I leave here."

"Yes." Vivian nodded. "Tell the principal that Clay Carson told you about the job. You can tell him about me, but Clay went to school with him and that will carry more weight. They need a full-time sub, and you can probably start next week."

"I can't believe how well this is working out. You will call me when I need to do anything else about the child support stuff?"

"I will." They walked to the door of the office, and Vivian laid her hand on Adelyn's shoulder. Her silky black hair hung loose down her back, shining against her white satin blouse. "And I will call you tomorrow and let you know what Lucas says about lodgings."

"Are you like this with everyone that comes in here?"

"I try to be." Vivian stopped and looked around the cream-colored walls of the office, her law degree and diplomas displayed in expensive modern frames behind her desk. "God has been much more gracious to me than I deserve, and so have the people of this town. I'm trying to learn from their example and do the same to others." She turned the doorknob and opened the door. "Of course, when I found out you are a friend of my favorite sister-in-law, I wanted to help even more."

*T*wo hours later, Adelyn put her palm over her growling stomach and slid behind the wheel of her car. *Lord, I know my attitude was bad this morning when I started out, and you have blessed me so much in spite of it. Thank you, God, for being good to me.*

She looked across the parking lot to the entrance of the elementary school with the catwalk running like a maze along the outside of one building to the next. The now familiar Carson the Alligator statue stood proudly in the manicured grassy area between the school and the parking lot. Marigolds and ornamental kale were planted all around the statue. *I'm going to be working there next week.* It still didn't seem real; it was even better than Vivian said. The state had approved an emergency teaching certificate allowing the school district to hire her for the open second-grade position. She would work on the last few hours needed to finish her degree over the next year while earning a teacher's salary instead of a substitute salary.

The principal had to run all the background checks and get her references from Shreveport, but that would all come back fine. She filled out the enormous application, interviewed, and then actually took a tour of the school, including the four-year-old kindergarten where Hazie May would enroll tomorrow. Her stomach growled again, and she looked in her wallet. A small knot of panic gnawed at her gut. She had two hundred dollars and needed work clothes. She couldn't show up in her blue jeans and LSU tee-shirt on her first day of work. She backed out of the parking lot and pulled onto the street.

Oh man, and Hazie May needed school clothes too. They had plenty of clothes back in Shreveport. Should she get Hazie May and drive back to get their things? If she picked up Hazie May and grabbed a sandwich from the apartment, they could be on the road by two, get their things from her old place and drive back by tonight. She hadn't spoken to anyone from her past life since they snuck away. Undoubtedly, she could get in and out of a city that size without Zane knowing about it. Plus, what would he be able to do? He threatened to do a lot of things during the divorce, but all he'd really done since she left him was bully her, scare her. She was not scared anymore.

She stopped at the red light and glanced at the surrounding vehicles. Sidney's red truck or the tow truck were nowhere in sight. He could have at least called and said he wasn't coming. Last night had been a mistake, a big mistake. She had too much on her plate to deal with a man who didn't have the common courtesy to let her know he wasn't going to keep an appointment. He hadn't forgotten about the law visit or just blew her off. No, he wasn't like that. Something came up. That was understandable, but to simply not show up. No, she had one child to raise. The last thing she needed was a man that was too childish to keep his promises or the manners to explain why he didn't. He was obviously at work somewhere. Why else would he have gotten the tow truck this morning? But there was no excuse for not calling.

She wasn't mad, well; she was a little. She would keep her emotions about Sidney Madison to herself. Fiona was a gem. She would not whine to her about Sidney. No, she needed friends here in Carson's Bayou. Sidney could be a friend, had been a friend, but a pattern in his behavior was emerging. She didn't have the time or the patience to play games with him. He wanted to keep his distance, fine. He could do that. She would pay him back for everything once she started earning a paycheck.

Fiona was turning into a much more reliable friend, and now Vivian Wade was in her corner as well. Adelyn pulled into the paved drive leading to what Hazie May called Fiona's mansion on the big hill. Things would work out. She could be strong. She was strong. She didn't need Sidney Madison's broad shoulders to lean on. The anger in her belly died a little as memories of his lips against hers, the husky voice saying her name in the moonlight shadows, and his spicy aftershave tickling her nose as she leaned into him attacked her thoughts. No, she stopped her car in the driveway and pulled in a deep, cleansing breath. No, she would not allow herself to pine after a man who did not have the same feelings for her. She ran her finger along her lower lip. Even a man as wonderful as Sidney Madison.

*S*he was planning on coming back. She had to be. Her clothes were still in the apartment. Sidney pushed his fingers through his hair and looked out of the garage doors again, willing Adelyn's little car to pull into the lot. It had taken over an hour to detour behind the college and weave back through town this morning to get to the wreck. Everyone and their grandma were trying to cut down those same little narrow streets, already clogged with school traffic. When he finally made it to where he was going, it took another hour to get the truck loaded and back to the shop. Adelyn wasn't there, but that was understandable. He didn't know how long a lawyer visit normally lasted, but it was noon, nothing to be concerned about.

He returned to the wreck to get the second vehicle, the totaled one, and brought it back. The insurance would definitely consider it unfixable, but they couldn't leave it on the highway. The second trip to the scene was a little quicker, the traffic clearing, but people were still wanting to stand around and talk about what happened. He didn't engage in the conversations, but he did have to wait to get the contact information of the car and towing forms signed. Time wasted.

Sidney finally pulled the tow truck up at the garage for the second time. He looked at his watch, 2:00. She still wasn't back. He fished his cell phone from the floorboard of the tow truck and climbed out, slamming the door. Shoving the phone in his back pocket, he slid behind the wheel of his pickup and stuck the keys in the ignition. He could run over to the law office and make sure everything was okay. No, he eased the keys back out of the ignition and flopped back against the seat. She wouldn't still be there, and driving around town looking for her gave off a creepy vibe. Sending a text would have to do. *Sorry I missed the appointment. How did it go?* That had been three hours ago. The next two texts still didn't get a response. She wouldn't have left him without taking her clothes, even if it was only a couple of things. Where was she?

The muscles in his shoulders knotted, and the idea he refused to believe pushed forward into his brain. Had that no-good husband of hers found her and somehow talked her into going back with him? Or worse, had he taken her back with him against her will? And Hazie May. He rubbed his fingers across his forehead, slowing his thoughts. Adelyn left Hazie May with Fiona. He pulled his phone out for the thirty-thousandth time and dialed his sister. Her voice mail politely told him she could not take his call and to try again later.

Forget the creepy stalker vibe. If that husband had taken her, and he fumbled around here being wishy washy about looking for her, he would never forgive himself. He sat up and pulled in a deep breath, his eyes looking up at the dark, empty apartment above the garage. He shoved the keys in the ignition and cranked his truck. This woman meant something to him, more than a casual friend, like he had been trying to convince himself. She needed him, and he let her down—again. He pulled onto the street and headed toward the law office. It might already be closed, but if that husband had taken her, her car might still be in the lot.

He hurried across town, driving faster than he ever had. The law office was closed as he expected, the parking lot was empty. Now what? He pulled back onto the street. He had given Adelyn her mother's business card yesterday when he told her about the woman being in town. His eyes narrowed, trying to remember the phone number on the glossy card, but it was no good. The numbers wouldn't come into his brain. He drove past the Bayou Bean, eyes searching the rows of cars parked on the street, then over to the park. A sick feeling rose in his throat and he made a loop through the nearby hospital parking lot.

She was gone. Really gone, without a word. Her car was gone, so she had probably just left. She might have gotten bad news from the lawyer and decided to take her mother up on her offer. She obviously couldn't count on him to help her.

He pulled onto the side of the road near the snowball stand, already closed down for the day. The black trash barrel near the tiny metal building with the sliding window was full of Styrofoam cups, all empty and stained with different colors, dripping down and washing away with the continual mist of rain. What now? He could go back to the garage, get to work, continue with life like he had been doing for all of his adult life before he found her on the side of the road. He lay his head back on the truck seat and closed his eyes. No, he couldn't. No use pretending. He wanted, no—he needed this woman in his life. Why was he so slow on the uptake? Why did it take something like this to get him to open his pig-headed eyes? He needed a plan and one formulated as he headed back to the garage.

He sat back up and started the truck engine. She was gone, but he would find her. He knew her mother's name and the town she lived in. He would start there. If her mother didn't know anything, he would go to Shreveport. She hadn't disappeared off the face of the planet. He would find her and explain. Explain that he wanted her, needed her in his life, and pray that he hadn't ruined that spark of feeling from her he was sure he had seen last night.

He pulled into the street and headed back to the garage. First, he needed to try to figure out her mother's address. He would search online, and maybe call Callie if he couldn't figure it out on his own. She was good at snooping around in things. Before the day was over, he needed to be on the road trying to find Adelyn. He pulled in a slow breath. *Calm down and think. Head to the garage, find her mother's address, formulate some kind of plan to talk Adelyn into coming back.* He could do this.

CHAPTER FIFTEEN

*A*delyn pulled into her usual parking spot beside the garage and hurried around to the back passenger's side to unbuckle Hazie May.

"Can I carry my bag?" Hazie May kicked her cowboy boots against the car booster seat, waiting for her mother to unlock her seat belt.

"Yes, that will be fine."

"Can I show Sidney my new clothes?"

"Sure." Adelyn released the buckle and pulled it from across her daughter's chest. "I know he will want to see them."

"Can I tell him about starting big girl school?"

"Of course."

"Can I bring Peter into the apartment out of the rain?"

"No." Adelyn grinned down at her daughter as she climbed from the back seat. "Peter is just fine under the overhang of the garage." She handed the bag of clothes to Hazie May and retrieved the other three bags from the back seat. "Now hurry up before the rain starts again."

Adelyn nudged the car door shut with her hip and looked

at the garage. Sidney made his way across the lot to where she and Hazie May stood. "Are you okay?" Adelyn stared at Sidney's stooped shoulders and sluggish gait. "You look like you are coming down with a cold or something."

"No, I'm fine. I was just getting ready to go look for you." Sidney reached over and took the bags from Adelyn's arms. "Here, let me tote those."

Adelyn handed Sidney the bags and followed along behind. Hazie May chatted like a magpie all the way up the stairs and into the apartment. "I got three new dresses and some leggings and some underwear with stars on them."

"Why don't you spread everything out on the bed while I fix us all something to drink?" Adelyn said to Hazie May. She took the bags from Sidney's arms and set them on the dresser nearby. "You want coffee, Coke, or tea?" she asked over her shoulder, walking to the kitchen area.

"Uh." Sidney looked from the bed to Adelyn. "I'll take whatever you're having."

Adelyn pulled a couple of glasses from the cabinet and a plastic cup for Hazie May. "Let's have tea then." She listened while Hazie May showed Sidney all of her new clothes from the thrift stores and Good Will, including her six-pack of underwear and socks from Target. "Okay, little girl. You have talked Mr. Sidney's ear off. It's time to let him and me catch up. You can look at that new princess book I got you."

She settled the child on a pillow in the bed with the book and returned to the kitchen. "I waited for you this morning," she said, sliding a glass of tea across the little table in his direction. "When you didn't show, I went on without you."

"I am so sorry about that." Sidney wrapped his hand around the glass and pulled it in front of him. "Traffic was backed up and I couldn't make it through to the wreck."

"That's understandable." Adelyn put the tea pitcher back in the fridge and returned to the table. "But not letting me know you weren't coming is not understandable." She lowered herself into the chair and looked at Sidney. "You could have called me and told me what was going on."

"I did." Sidney's eyes shot up from where he was staring at the glass. "I mean, I didn't call, but I texted and told you I wasn't going to make it."

"Are you sure?" Adelyn raised an eyebrow. "Because I didn't get a text. Believe me. I checked my phone several times, hoping I had missed your call."

"I'm sure." Sidney pulled his phone from his back pocket and scrolled backwards through to the text he sent earlier that day. "Oh—well." He slid the phone across for Adelyn to look at the screen. "I guess the service is bad out there. It didn't go through." He watched Adelyn's face as she read the text and the following messages. "I really thought I let you know. I should have checked my phone again, but I was so aggravated with the traffic, and missing the meeting with the lawyer." He slumped back in the chair. "It never occurred to me you didn't get the message. I'm truly sorry."

"It's okay." Adelyn slid the phone back across the table. "I wasn't mad. Well, I was a little mad, but mostly disappointed. I turned my phone off when I got to the lawyer's office so I wouldn't be bothered in case you finally decided to let me know what was going on. So yeah, I guess I was a little mad." She picked up her tea glass and took a sip. "But everything worked out. I met Fiona's sister-in-law. She is a lawyer there and said she would be working with me instead of the other guy."

"She's a nice person. Fiona says she's smart as a whip." Sidney pulled his legs in from where he had sprawled them in front of him and sat up a little straighter. "What did you find out? If Hazie May is getting ready to go to school, I'm assuming it's good news."

"Great news." Adelyn looked across the room at her

daughter and then back at Sidney. "I actually have a job at the elementary school, and Hazie May will start four-year-old kindergarten there, too. It was truly an answer to prayer." Her brow furrowed, and she looked at Sidney's down-turned face. "What's wrong? This means I won't have to mooch off of you anymore. It also means I can start teaching, really teaching, like I've wanted to ever since I was in college."

"I'm happy for you." Sidney looked across the table at Adelyn, his heart in his eyes. It had taken quite a while to find her mother's address. He was on his way to the truck when he heard them talking. The relief that washed over him when he saw Adelyn getting Hazie May out of her car a few minutes ago had literally left him weak in the knees. *Get your act together and stop just staring at her like some kind of lovesick puppy.* He glanced over at Hazie May, flipping through the giant fairy tale book spread across her lap. Now was the time. The Lord had answered his prayer and brought them back to him. It was time to say what was on his mind and in his heart.

"I need to talk to you about something, and it's something I'm not good at talking about." He rubbed his hand across his jaw. "When I got back, and you weren't here, and then you didn't come home, I kind of panicked." He blew out a puff of air and sat back in the chair. "At first I thought your husband may have taken you, or talked you into going back with him to Shreveport."

"Hmph. You definitely don't have to worry about that happening."

"Well, after I looked all over town and couldn't find your vehicle, I decided you had left town on your own." Sidney's eyes roamed around the room looking for the right words then settled on Adelyn's face, drawing courage from the expectant look in her eyes. "Here it is. When I realized you were gone, maybe gone for good, I saw the rest of my life without you in it." His voice dropped into a gravely whisper. "It wasn't good." He swallowed the knot in his throat. "I don't want to just be your friend. I want to be more than that."

Adelyn's eyes narrowed. Sidney watched her expression change, his heart pounding in his chest. "I'm not trying to rush into anything," he continued, the words gushing out. "We can keep being what we are. The thing is, I know you are the one for me. I was too stubborn to see that until I thought you were gone."

"Sidney."

"Now I know. It's you. Only you."

"Sidney." Adelyn's eyes softened. "I like you too. I like you a whole lot, but I was wrong to rush you like I did last night. I realize that now." She bit her bottom lip. "Plus, I did a lot of thinking today, and I've decided a few things myself."

The knot in Sidney's throat moved to his stomach. "Okay."

"So far, our friendship has been very one-sided. You have done all the giving, and I have done all the taking."

"But . . ."

"No." Adelyn reached across the table and placed her hand on Sidney's arm. "Listen to me. You don't know how grateful I am for you. You have truly been a lifesaver, a gift from God. I need, I desperately need to find some kind of equal footing. I stayed with Zane in a marriage based on bullying and fear because I believed I couldn't make it without him." Her lips pushed up into a thoughtful smile. "That's not the way God intended marriage to be. After my meeting with Mother, I did a lot of praying. I decided that I'm not afraid anymore. I know God has a plan for me that is good."

"Adelyn." Sidney reached over and took her hand. "I think I'm part of that plan if you will give me another chance."

"You may be, Sidney. You probably are, but can't you see that I need to get my life together? Me. I need to know that I can have a life worth living with my daughter before I bring someone else into it."

"So." Sidney longed to reach across the table and brush the wisp of hair away from Adelyn's cheek, to hold her face in his hands, to tell her he would fix everything for her, but he didn't have that right. "What does this mean for us?"

"For one thing, it means I'm staying in Carson's Bayou, but I'm looking for my own place. Vivian said her husband is on this committee that helps people in my situation find decent places to live that they can afford. She said it may take a little time, but I'm supposed to get an application for their next building project. They are looking at new applicants now." She slipped her hand from Sidney's. "I need to continue to stay here, but with my job at the school, I can really start to pay rent and help pay for food and stuff."

"And us?"

"I want us to be there too, but not as a damsel in distress and the knight in shining armor. I want us to be two people who are on equal footing."

"I've never seen me as your rescuer," Sidney said, pictures of losing Hazie May in the park racing through his mind. "I'm definitely not a hero, and I don't see you as a victim either. You are striking out on your own with no help, and you're making it work."

"Because of you, Sid." Adelyn reached up and tucked the strand of hair behind her ear. "Maybe we could go out again. Start over. I'm not going anywhere, so we can take it slow and see how things work out." She glanced across the room at Hazie May, then back at Sidney. "She's been through so much these past few weeks. I think slow will be best for all of us."

"I'm not going to let you down again." The worry of losing Adelyn lost some of its grip and Sidney's face softened. "I'm going to be who you need me to be."

"I need you to be you, Sidney. That's good enough. Actually, that's more than good enough."

Sidney smiled and picked up his tea glass. No, he would do better. She was right. She needed to get a job and have some security on her own, but he also wanted her to be able to rely on him, truly rely on him. There was no use telling her that. Anybody could say those things. He would show her. Like she said, she would be here. He would be here. It was time to come out of his shell and start showing her the man he could be, would be—for her.

CHAPTER SIXTEEN

"You don't have to do this." Adelyn looked at Sidney, her eyes twinkling. A mischievous grin stretched across her face. "She will understand."

"I don't mind." Sidney stared at his reflection in the mirror. He turned to the side, and the giant green alligator tail swept across the floor of the apartment. The padded green belly of the suit stuck out front, and he grinned. "Absolutely ridiculous. Besides, with the head on, nobody will know it's me, anyway."

"Ha." Adelyn laughed and ran her hand along the bright green spikes going down the back of the Carson's Bayou Elementary school mascot. "Hazie May will tell everyone within earshot who's in the gator suit. You can count on that."

"That's fine, too." Sidney lifted the enormous cartoon alligator head and placed it on his shoulders. He peered through the mesh screen at Adelyn. "I'm glad she asked me to help her out."

"She loves you. Of course she asked you." Adelyn stared at the eight-foot-tall alligator, tapping her fingers to her lips.

"You know that. I don't want you to think you have to do this though. I know it's a little out of your comfort zone. I would wear it, except I have to work at the second-grade booth."

"I really don't mind." Sidney lifted the alligator head back off his shoulders and shook out his hair, where it was already sticking to his head. "It's going to get hot in there, but at least it's been a little cooler here lately. I haven't gone to a Heritage Days Festival at the school since Callie was in sixth grade and Nana needed help setting up her Mayhaw jelly booth." He reached back and groped for the zipper at the neck of the costume. "Can you help me get out of this thing? I'll keep it down in the office until Saturday so you won't have to worry about it up here."

Adelyn stepped over and found the zipper, tugging it down. "That's a good idea. Hazie May won't be able to keep her hands off it if it stays in the apartment." She watched Sidney wrestle himself out of the costume. "You make a huge alligator. If you were any taller, you wouldn't fit in there." She looked up at his six-foot-tall frame and broad shoulders. "It's kind of snug everywhere, isn't it?"

"I'll manage for a day," Sidney said, tugging his blue jeans back into place where the suit pushed them up. "But if this was a routine thing, I would have to get the suit let out in the straddle." He folded the bulky alligator body over his arm and looked at Adelyn. "Can you get the head? We need to get over to the meeting at the homeless shelter, or you are going to be late."

"Let me grab my purse." Adelyn slid her bag onto her shoulder and picked up the gator head off the bed. Six weeks ago, she had turned in the application Vivian had given her requesting assistance in finding a home. Since then, she and Hazie May had continued to live in the apartment, but everything else about their lives had changed considerably.

She started to work as the new second-grade teacher, and

Hazie May enrolled the same day in the four-year-old kindergarten class. She received her first check from the school two weeks ago and opened a checking and savings account at the local bank. She proudly paid part of the repair bill on the car, gave Sidney rent money on the apartment, and bought groceries.

"You don't have to pay rent on this place," Sidney said, looking down at the money Adelyn had placed in his hand. "You've been cooking, cleaning, and helping me with the office stuff. I told you that would take care of the rent."

"This is not nearly enough money to cover what a real renter would bring in," Adelyn said, shoving Sidney's hand and the money back in his direction. "The cleaning I do is only the messes me and Hazie May make. You know good and well what I do in that office doesn't amount to a hill of beans." She squeezed his hand, the warmth of his touch sending a slight shiver across the back of her neck. "Besides, I need to do this. It makes me feel like I'm taking responsibility for my own life."

"Alright." Sidney looked down at Adelyn's face as a tenderness warmed his voice. "But promise me that if you need this back, you won't hesitate to ask for it."

"I promise." Adelyn drug her teeth over her lower lip and stared into Sidney's eyes. She blinked a couple of times and let go of his hand, getting control of the longing washing over her. "Your sister hooked me up with clothes from the Good Will store and a few thrift stores within driving distance of Carson's Bayou, remember? We are set on clothes and shoes for a while."

Adelyn followed Sidney down the outside steps from the apartment to the garage. The memories of the past six weeks flooded her thoughts. Things had settled into a comfortable routine since their talk that day she saw Vivian at the law office, and then went to the thrift stores with Fiona. Sidney would still come eat breakfast with them every morning, as always, but as soon as they were done, she and Hazie May headed out the door to the school. The first day she came home and found the breakfast dishes washed, and a crock pot full of chili on the counter. She protested, but Sidney insisted he was only doing his part now that she was a working woman.

"I've been cleaning up after myself for a long time," Sidney said, ignoring Adelyn's protests. "And don't thank me for cooking supper until you actually taste it." He pulled a family size bag of Fritos from the cabinet. "You may not be able to eat it."

Despite his warning, the chili turned out great. Sidney would have something in the crock pot about two times a week. He offered to eat a sandwich or fix his own dinner when he got home the other nights, but Adelyn assured him she could still cook supper for them and hold down her job.

The refrigerator was now decorated with artwork from Hazie May's school projects. Peter, the cat, was an official member of their family. A frown creased Adelyn's brow. Family. Where had that come from? Sidney was doing exactly what Adelyn had asked him to do. He was behaving like a friend, a dependable, wonderful friend. A friend who made her insides do flip-flops every time she got within three feet of him.

They had not gone out on another date. She had sort of insinuated that was how she wanted it to be when they had talked that day. Even so, they had gone to the park a few times with Hazie May, and ridden to church together every Sunday. Sidney had also set up a couple of chairs in the back of the garage. She and the child spent most of their afternoons there while Sidney worked on the vehicles. Even though they had not officially gone out on another date, they were spending all of their time together.

One of Adelyn's greatest surprises had been the day a Zydeco song came on the radio. "Hazie May, may I have this dance?" He scooped the child up and danced all over the back of the garage, moving his feet perfectly as Hazie May giggled and bobbed her head to the snappy Cajun music.

"Now dance with Momma," Hazie May said, clapping her hands together when he plopped her down after the song. "She can't dance like you, can you, Momma?"

"Well, no. I can't," Adelyn said, her eyes stretched wide. "You are just full of surprises, Mr. Madison."

"Madame." Sidney bent low in front of the lawn chair and extended his hand as "It's Your Love" by Tim McGraw came on the radio. "May I have this dance?"

"I'm not much of a dancer."

"Dance, Momma," Hazie May said, clapping her hands together. "Sid knows how to dance. You don't have to do anything but hang on."

"She's right," Sidney said, winking at Adelyn. "Just hang on."

Adelyn took Sidney's hand and breathed in a deep sigh. His arms wrapped around her, guiding her around the back of the garage. Hazie May picked up Peter and began dancing around nearby. The whole thing was so right, so normal. "Where did you learn to dance?" Adelyn asked, looking up as Sidney glided her across the concrete floor.

"My Nana." Sidney swayed and moved to the music perfectly, taking Adelyn with him as the love song gradually drew to a close. "Sunday afternoons we would push the coffee table out of the way, and Nana would teach us how to dance. I never knew my grandfather, but apparently he and Nana used to love to cut a rug. Sometimes the neighbors would come over and we would go in the backyard, make ice cream, and dance all afternoon."

"Sidney Madison, you are full of surprises." Adelyn

looked up into his face and they danced their way back to her chair.

"Good surprises, I hope."

"Yes, very good."

*S*idney listened to Lucas Wade explain to Adelyn how the building project would work. Out of the fourteen applicants who had applied for the house, only four actually met the qualifications set forth by the community church council. Out of those four, the council had chosen Adelyn. He was happy for her. He really was. Since she started working and having her own income, she had literally blossomed like those morning glories in his backyard that Nana had loved so much. The worried look that often troubled her face when she first appeared in Carson's Bayou seldom appeared on her brow anymore. For that, he was truly grateful.

He loved Adelyn. This was certain, beyond a shadow of a doubt. If it was up to him, Adelyn would stay right there in the apartment until he had enough time to show her how much she meant to him, how much he wanted to be the man in her life. That was not what Adelyn wanted, though, so he would be happy. He'd be happy she was moving if it made her happy. At least she would still be in Carson's Bayou and was not moving away to where her mother lived. It might take longer to win her heart once she moved out, but he would win it. He would do whatever it took to make that happen.

Building the house would take a little while anyway. They had to find land to build on. A lot of people the council had built houses for in the past already had the land, but not all of them. This extra step took time, but from what he knew of the Wade brothers, once the land was obtained, they would waste no time in getting the house built.

Sidney had met both the brothers back when Fiona started working for Langston, but their reputations as businessmen were well known. Plus, Lucas Wade had worked on these building projects for people down on their luck through the church council for a few years now. What he was able to accomplish with the volunteers and donations from the churches and other charitable organizations in the area was truly amazing.

A slight prickle in the back of Sidney's brain made him frown. If he was willing to step out on faith, leave his fears of failure behind, could God use him like that? He was not a Wade, did not have the resources they had, or their outgoing personalities either. What could God possibly do with him? *You won't know if you don't step out.* A voice whispered in his head. *Step out.*

CHAPTER SEVENTEEN

"*S*he was in the jumping house and we were waiting for her to come out," Fiona said, swallowing the fear in the edge of her voice. "But when all the kids came out, she wasn't with them."

"I'm sure she has wandered off with someone she knows," the policeman said, looking from Fiona to Adelyn. "Don't worry. We will find her."

Adelyn wrung her hands together, pushing down the panic rising in her throat. Her ex-husband had come to Carson's Bayou. That had to be it. Anybody else would have brought her to the second-grade booth, to her mother. Why had she risked sending the paperwork to him for the child support? She had a job now. She could make it without that money. She should have gone back to the lawyer's office the day she got the teaching position to stop the process for getting the back payments Zane owed for child support. Why had she let her need to feel strong and in control override her good sense?

"Ma'am."

"What?" Adelyn blinked and looked at the officer staring at her, waiting for an answer.

"He asked if you have a picture on your phone you could text him so he can send it out to get more help to search for Hazie May," Langston said, looking at Adelyn's pale face. "She's probably with Sidney. Try not to worry."

"Um, yeah." Adelyn ignored the queasy feeling in her stomach and pulled her phone from her pocket. "Here." She opened her screen and pulled up a picture, then handed the phone to Langston. She looked past the policeman through the crowd of people wandering from one place to the other. Langston was right. Hazie May had probably left the jumpy house and went to find Sidney. She was so proud that he was the alligator today. She had probably seen him and forgotten she was supposed to stay with Fiona and Langston. "Has anyone seen Sidney?" she asked, turning and searching the crowd of people around them.

Adelyn turned back to the policeman. "There's something I need to tell you. I have a restraining order on my husband, but I don't think he knows I'm in Carson's Bayou. He lives in Shreveport." *But he might know. He might have my baby.* "His name is Zane Jones."

The policeman paused from talking into his cell phone and looked at Adelyn. "Has he threatened to take the child, or ever tried to take her before?"

"No, but he showed up at her school. That's one of the reasons I left Shreveport. He kept showing up in places he knew we would be." Adelyn's eyes darted from the policeman to Langston and Fiona. "He never came too close, but he made sure I saw him. It was like he was taunting me."

The policeman took a description of Zane Jones from Adelyn, then left them to search for Hazie May.

Adelyn pulled in a deep, quaking gulp of air. "We need to start looking for her, too."

"I'm going to the stage and make an announcement for everyone to search," Langston said. "Don't worry, Adelyn. We'll find her."

Fiona's hand slipped into Adelyn's as they watched Langston's shoulders disappear through the crowd toward the stage. The cheerful Cajun music played on. Adelyn closed her eyes. Sidney. Sidney would help her find Hazie May. She needed to get to Sidney.

"Let's pray," Fiona said, taking Adelyn's other hand and bowing her head.

Fiona's urgent prayer for Hazie May's return filled Adelyn's ears. The music stopped and the sound of Langston's voice over the sound system quieted the crowd, asking everyone to help find her missing daughter. *God, please, please bring me my baby. I understand you are with her wherever she is. Please protect her and bring her back to me.*

Adelyn lifted her head as Fiona finished her prayer and said amen. "I've got to start looking. I can't stand here and wait." She looked down at her phone. "I need to call Sidney, but he left his phone in the truck. He couldn't get it out of his jeans pocket while he was wearing the alligator costume."

"Don't worry." Fiona followed Adelyn as they started walking through the crowd of people. "He'll hear Langston's announcement and get in touch with us. He's probably with Hazie May right now, looking for you."

"I hope so," Adelyn said, blinking back the tears threatening to spill down her face. "I've told her so many times that she shouldn't wander off, but she gets excited and forgets."

"I feel awful," Fiona said, looking around at the people going from one attraction to the next, the sounds of the festival slowly starting again. "We were right there at the jumpy house. I don't know how she got away from us."

"It's not your fault," Adelyn said, eyes scanning every child within her line of vision. "It's mine. If Zane has taken her, it is all my fault."

"She is okay, Adelyn. I'm sure we will find her."

Fiona's words sounded distant as Adelyn continued to walk through the crowd. Fiona didn't know her ex-husband, didn't know what she had left behind. *Dear God, please let them find my child.*

S o much for a cool fall day. A bead of sweat trickled down the side of Sidney's face. He longed to take the alligator head off for just a second and push the brown curls plastered to his forehead back, to inhale a couple of breaths of fresh air. As usual, almost the entire town of Carson's Bayou turned out to support the school for the Heritage Day Festival. This year, the money raised would go to the music department to replace several worn out band instruments. Sidney weaved his way through the crowds of people wandering from booth to booth along the blocked off street in front of the school. A local group was set up in the center of the parking lot playing Cajun music, and several people of all ages were dancing. The sweet smell of funnel cakes combined with the spicy aroma of jambalaya, sausage dogs, and other foods from the vendors penetrated the alligator head. Sidney's stomach growled.

The fire department had a truck set up on the other side of the parking lot. Blaze Carson, one of the local firefighters, was letting the kids try on the gear and look at the truck. Fiona and Langston had taken Hazie May over to see the fire truck a while back, volunteering to walk the child around the festival so she wouldn't have to stay with Adelyn who was running a booth selling cakes, pies and other baked goods for the second-grade class. Sidney stopped and a couple holding a little boy, probably around three, walked up wanting a picture of their son with Carson the alligator. He pulled a helium-filled balloon from his hand and offered the string to the boy.

"Will you let the alligator hold you, Justice?" the woman asked, tying the ribbon around the child's arm as the attached balloon bobbed up and down. "He's a nice alligator."

Sidney held his arms out for the child, like he had already done dozens of times today to pick up other children. The child leaned back away from the gigantic alligator and buried his face in his mother's tee-shirt. Sidney waited. The dad eventually stood beside him with the child on his opposite hip while the mother snapped a few pictures.

The couple left and six upper elementary kids walked up. Sidney passed out his last balloons and looked up at the cloudless fall sky. It was time for a water break. He glanced up and down the street, then behind him to the school parking lot. He slowly weaved through the crowds to the end of the barricaded street where the festival goers parked their cars. A cooler full of water waited for him in the back of his truck. He could slip off the gator head, drink a bottle of water, and find a bathroom before getting another bundle of balloons to pass out. The festival had started at ten, and from the look of the sun beating down overhead, he had been wandering around, letting people get their picture made with the school mascot and giving them a free balloon for at least two hours. Only for Hazie May would he be doing this.

He walked between the rows of vehicles to where his truck was parked nearby, slipping the green gloves with the orange claws from his hands.

"Daddy, I don't want to get in your car. I thought we were going to find Momma."

Sidney dropped the gloves in the back of the truck bed and turned, searching the parking lot for the familiar voice.

"We'll go look for your mother in a minute, Zella. Right now, I need you to get in the car."

Three rows over, Sidney spotted a man opening up the door of a black Corvette and Hazie May pulling against him, struggling to break free. The man jerked the stuffed animal from the child's hand and tossed it in the car, continuing to hang onto her arm. "Get in the car with your teddy bear and we will go get some ice cream."

"No, Daddy." Hazie May's voice sobbed. "I don't want to go with you. I want Momma."

Sidney's footsteps closed in on the man as what was happening filled his head. Zane Jones. Adelyn's husband had found them, probably because of the child support action. Adelyn said she had filed a restraining order against this guy after the divorce when he had started harassing her. He had always made sure he stayed far enough away to keep from being brought in by the police. Apparently, that was changing now.

"Hey." Sidney stepped up to the man, the padded middle of the alligator costume pushing against the guy's side. The man lifted Hazie May, now crying and struggling to get out of his grip. He wedged himself between Sidney and the child. "Put her down," Sidney growled.

"Listen, alligator." The man shoved Hazie May into the front seat of the car and turned to Sidney. "This girl is my daughter, and she's mad because it's time to go home." He grinned, an arrogant glint in his eyes. "Go back to playing in your little costume, and I won't call the cops on you for harassing me and my daughter."

"Sid," Hazie May wailed. She stood in the seat, leaning out of the car. "I don't want to go with Daddy. He said we were going to find Momma, but we didn't. I want Momma."

"Give me the child," Sidney said, looking through the mask at the man whose face was glaring at him, only inches away. "I know who you are, and that you are not supposed to have the little girl."

"Alright, alright." Zane held up both hands. "Calm down. This is a big misunderstanding." He stepped back away from Sidney, his body pushing the car door closed.

"Give me the child." Sidney stepped closer, raising his arms to lift the ridiculous alligator head off his shoulders.

Sidney placed his hands on either side of the mascot's head to remove it. Zane swiftly pushed him backwards onto the pavement, then turned to open the car door. "I don't know who you are," he yelled, staring at Sidney laying in the street, the alligator tail bent to one side and the potbelly stuffing on the other, the enormous head still in place, "but you need to mind your own business."

Sidney struggled against the bulky suit and heavy head of the costume, but finally stood. Zane opened the door to the Corvette, but Hazie May kicked and screamed, slowing his progress. Zane shoved the child across the seat and slid behind the steering wheel of the car, a smug grin on his face.

Sidney could not let this man take Hazie May. All other thoughts fled from his mind as the guy pulled the car door close. Sidney dove at the car and his hands grabbed for Zane's clothing. He shoved the alligator head off the rest of the way with his right hand while the fingers of his left hand clutched the man's starched white shirt. Zane stood from the car, pulling against Sidney. The mask fell to the ground and fresh air surrounded Sidney just as Zane's fist landed against his jaw.

Hazie May's screams continued behind the men. Sidney staggered backwards with the force of the blow, dragging Zane with him, refusing to let go of him as Zane attempted to jerk free. Feet running across the parking lot mixed with shouting filled Sidney's ears. His fist connected with Hazie

May's father's face. He dropped like a rock, unconscious, his face landing on Sidney's tail.

Somewhere from the festival area, Sidney heard Langston Wade's voice over the loudspeakers. "If you see her, please bring her to the second-grade baked goods booth."

CHAPTER EIGHTEEN

*S*idney looked down at the pads of his fingers, black and smudged. The stains of the fingerprint ink somehow seemed fitting for what happened today. He followed the deputy to the cell and waited. The man slid the metal bars shut behind him, the clanging metal door echoing up and down the hall. At least Nana wasn't around to witness this. What would Fiona and Callie say when they found out he was in jail? It didn't matter. At least Hazie May was safe. He had to remember that. That's what mattered.

The police had shoved him, alligator suit and all, into one car, and Zane Jones into a second car. The cars pulled away, Sidney watching through the glass as another policeman talked to Hazie May. That had been two hours ago. Her small face, streaked with tears, eyes stretched wide, clinging to the teddy bear her father had thrown in his car to lure her into his trap, was seared into his mind.

He had never even been to the Carson's Bayou police department, much less been arrested. On TV, the prisoners always got a phone call. Who would he call? Certainly not Adelyn. What would she say when she found out he was in jail for punching out her ex-husband? Probably that he was just like Zane Jones, just like his own father after all.

He reached behind him, trying to find the zipper so he could get out of the alligator suit. Where was the head of this thing, anyway? He would have to buy a new one for the school. This one had been put through the ringer, not to mention that he had sweated in it like a pig.

"Hey, you're the alligator that punched out that dentist." A man pushed a broom along the concrete floor outside of the cell. "Was that guy stealing your kid?"

"My friend's daughter," Sidney said, walking over to the cell bars, the green tail dragging along behind him on the not too clean concrete floor. "Can you unzip this thing for me? It's hot as blue blazes in this suit."

"You got on clothes under that gator suit?" the man asked, leaning the broom against the wall near the cell. "If you're naked under there, you better leave it on."

"I'm dressed," Sidney said, voice flat. He turned his back to the bars and waited while the man unzipped the costume. "How do you know about the fight?"

"It's on Facebook and Tic Toc and all over the place," the man said. He grinned, showing a big gap in his two top teeth. "Funniest thing I've seen in a long time."

"Did you say the other guy is a dentist?" Sidney stepped out of the alligator costume and tossed it on the cot behind him. His tee-shirt was damp with perspiration. If they could salvage the costume, he would at least have to get the thing dry cleaned or something before he took it back to the school.

"That's what it's saying on the video." The man reached into his jeans pocket and pulled out his phone. "Here, look at this."

Sidney watched the video showing him hitting the ground, flopping around like a beached whale in the cartoonish alligator costume while trying to get back up, then charging the Corvette, green tail dragging the pavement behind him. It finally ended with Zane Jones being punched out and face planting on the alligator tail. Hazie May, crying in the background, witnessed the entire scene.

The janitor continued to rattle on about the fight and the video, but Sidney's mind kept going back to Hazie May. He could have handled that better. Why didn't he take off the stupid alligator head to start with? He could have made the guy listen to him instead of charging him like a mad bull. What would Adelyn do? She would probably be gone from the apartment when he got out of jail. He wouldn't blame her if she left Carson's Bayou all together. The janitor finally ran out of things to say and picked his broom back up from where he had propped it. Sidney watched, his brow furrowed. "I need to make a phone call."

"You want me to go get the deputy for you?" the man asked, grinning at Sidney. "They should be about finished with that dentist you punched. He was cursing and ripping and giving them the what for. Between you and me, I don't blame you for punching him. Some people need to be punched every once in a while."

"Yeah. Can you go get the deputy for me?" Sidney watched the boney little man hurry back out of sight down the hall. Langston. He would call Langston. He needed to make sure Hazie May was okay and find out what he had to do to get out of jail.

"Someone's here to see you." A deputy in a khaki colored uniform and a crewcut walked down the hall and unlocked the cell door. "Follow me. Teelee said you want to make a phone call. I'll let you do that when you get through talking to your visitor."

Sidney followed the officer to an eight by eight room with a narrow table bolted to the floor. A metal folding chair sat on either side. Sidney sat in the chair facing the door. The deputy disappeared to get the visitor. Sidney's eyes roamed around the room, taking in the pale gray cinderblock walls. What if Adelyn left, never spoke to him again? She wanted stability for her and Hazie May. That's the main thing she needed from him, and where was he? He was in jail for beating up her ex. His back slumped against the metal chair, and he stared up at the fluorescent lights above his head. It seemed he was like his father after all, undependable, violent.

He was not right for Adelyn, and to pretend he was would only expose her and Hazie May to more disappointment. The weight of the decision landed on him like a boulder, crushing his heart, but even with the pain, this decision was the right thing to do. Adelyn would never want to talk to him again after today. Even if she forgave him for letting Hazie May be a part of such an ugly scene, he would not allow himself to step back into their lives. Adelyn deserved better than him, better than her ex. He loved her, but he was not the man for her. She needed somebody she could be proud of, not ashamed of.

The door opened, and Sidney looked up. His eyebrows rose as the woman sat down in the other chair. "What are you doing here?"

"I'm offering my services as your lawyer. After all, we both want what's best for Adelyn, don't we?"

"I know I do." Sidney's brow wrinkled, and he stared at the woman. "I think I'll wait and get my own lawyer," he said, watching the woman's mask of concern slip from her face. Her eyes narrowed into slits, and her lips drew into a thin line.

"Stay away from my daughter," Mrs. Swan said, pushing the chair back from the table. "She deserves better than you. So does my granddaughter. Don't be a home wrecker."

Sidney watched Adelyn's mother turn and leave the

room. Adelyn didn't trust her mother, and he was beginning to understand why. Zane Jones reminded him of an arrogant bull, forcing his will on others and stomping them down out of his way. Deborah Swan was more calculating; manipulative. Why was she in Carson's Bayou at the same time as the ex-husband? What was going on?

*W*hat do you mean he won't see me?" Adelyn stared at Langston, disbelief in her voice. "He's in jail for rescuing Hazie May from being kidnapped by her father," she said, running her fingers through the hair across the top of her head. "I need to talk to him. I need to thank him."

"I know, Adelyn, but all I can tell you is that he said he didn't want to see you." Langston stood outside of the apartment and looked down the steps to where Fiona waited in the truck. He turned back to Adelyn. "They are letting him out in the morning. Once he gets home, I'm sure you two can work this out."

"Did he say why he wouldn't see me?"

"No. He did say that your mother came by and asked if she could be his lawyer."

"My mother?" Adelyn's voice rose. She looked over her shoulder through the apartment door to where Hazie May lay sleeping in the bed. "I hope he turned her down."

"He did. Vivian is representing him. She said that since you have a restraining order against your ex-husband, and Sidney was trying to protect Hazie May, that he has nothing to worry about. She also said that your ex-husband is probably going to jail for this."

"Thank the Lord," Adelyn said, her voice back under

control, "but what is my mother doing back in Carson's Bayou? Why would she be trying to help Sidney?"

"I don't know, but Fiona and Vivian are looking into it." He smiled down at Adelyn. "That is, if you don't mind. We've kind of adopted you into the family, and we look out after our family."

"Thank you." Tears formed in the corners of Adelyn's eyes. "You and Fiona and Sidney have been more of a family to me than anyone has ever been, except for my dad." She reached up and wiped a tear from her cheek. "I don't know what's going on with Sidney, or what my mother may have told him, but I need to talk to him. He has got to know how grateful I am that he didn't let Zane take Hazie May."

"Just give him some time." Langston patted Adelyn on the shoulder. "Sidney is a very level-headed guy. He needs a little time to process what happened. It's not every day that a guy in an alligator suit gets thrown in jail for punching out a man. In Carson's Bayou that's hot news. He's probably embarrassed."

Adelyn thanked Langston and waved to Fiona as they drove away. Langston was right about Sidney being level-headed, but she didn't think he was embarrassed. Sidney didn't care what strangers thought about him. He wasn't wired that way. Something else was bothering him, and if she knew anything about him, she felt certain it had to do with her husband taking Hazie May. She had given him such a hard time that day he had lost her child at the park. When he missed the lawyer's appointment, he had put a wall up, pulling himself out of her life because he was worried about not being good enough.

Well, if Sidney Madison thought he could back out of her life that easily without a fight from her, he had better think again. Should she go to the jail this evening? Zane was there.

She did not want to risk running into him. Plus, she did not want to take Hazie May there.

She pushed the apartment door to where there was only a crack in the opening, then sat down on the stoop outside. The sky, dimming in the evening sun, was splattered with pinks and purples in a blue background. *Dear Lord, thank you for sending Sidney when you did to protect Hazie May. Lord, please open Sidney's eyes. Let him realize that he is a good man. Let him believe that you have made him a new creation through Christ; that he is not his father's son—but Your son. Forgive me, God. I can see now that me wanting to rely only on me is just as wrong as me relying completely on Zane. Help me to rely on You, Father, to trust the path you've put before me and the people You have put in it to help me. You have given me a love for Sidney, and I am ready to open my heart to him. I'm ready to rely on him as the man I love. Please, God, please don't let it be too late. I know I am always asking, and you are always giving. Please, open Sidney's eyes to see that he is the man for me.*

"Momma?" Hazie May pushed open the apartment door and rubbed her eyes with the back of her hands. "I'm hungry. Is Sid coming so we can eat?"

"He won't be eating with us tonight, honey, but we can go ahead and eat if you want to."

"Momma." Hazie May sat down on the stoop and pulled her knees up to her chest. "I was so scared today until I saw Sid coming up to the car." She eased her hand out and slipped it into Adelyn's. "Is it okay if I love Sidney more than Daddy?"

"It's okay, honey."

"I wish Sid was here."

"I do too, honey. I do too."

*a*delyn followed the officer down the narrow hall, dimly lit by a glowing florescent bulb above her head. After eating dinner and tucking Hazie May in bed, she had not been able to sit still. She had found the card her mother gave Sidney the other day and dialed her mother, needing to learn why she had been to see him. There was no answer, and she did not leave a message. Finally, after a lot of pacing, and almost waking her daughter up more than once, she called Fiona. "I know he said he didn't want to see me, but I want to see him." Adelyn stood on the steps outside of the apartment, careful to not wake her daughter. "Can you come watch Hazie May for a while? I won't be long."

Fiona showed up fifteen minutes later, and Adelyn left for the police station. "Are you going to be in there with us?" Adelyn asked the man as they stopped in front of the metal door.

"No, ma'am, not unless you want me to be." The officer looked at Adelyn, his hand on the doorknob.

"No, I would rather speak to Sidney alone."

"Then I will be right here. Knock when you're finished, and I will open the door."

Adelyn stepped through the opening and glanced around at the barren gray walls. Her gaze settled on Sidney, sitting in the metal chair on the other side of the scarred up wooden table.

"You shouldn't be here." Sidney stood, forehead wrinkled. "You didn't bring Hazie May here, did you?"

"No, of course not." Adelyn walked the two steps to the table and pulled out the metal chair. The scraping sound of the legs dragging across the concrete floor echoed through the empty room. "Are you okay?"

"I'm fine. You shouldn't be here."

Sidney sat back down, and Adelyn looked closer at his

face. "You've been hurt." She stepped around the table, forgetting the instructions the officer had given her about staying seated during the visit. Leaning down, she touched Sidney's face. Her fingers gently grazed the puffy area under his eye. His face turned into her hand and a rush of heat flushed her skin. "I'm sorry I've brought my messy life to your doorsteps."

Sidney's eyes closed as her hand caressed his cheek. He pulled in a ragged breath and opened them again. The old, distant look, a look Adelyn didn't know how to deal with, crept over his face. The wall was back up. "I'm fine," he mumbled. He reached up and pulled her hand from his face. "You have to stay on the other side of the table."

"You're doing it again." Adelyn swallowed back the tears clogging her throat. She stepped back and eased around the table. "Why do you keep shutting me out?"

"I'm in jail, Adelyn. You shouldn't be here. I asked you to stay away." Sidney's eyes darted away from Adelyn's stare. "This is no place for you."

"No place for me?" Adelyn's harsh laugh rang through the room. "I suppose you belong here?" Her eyes bulged, and she waved her arm around the room. "I suppose you get arrested all the time for punching out strangers? For rescuing children from their psycho fathers?"

"Adelyn." Sidney's voice remained calm, controlled. "Go home."

"You know what, Sidney Madison? You are in jail tonight because of me, but even when you get out of here tomorrow, you will still be in jail." Adelyn stared across the table at Sidney, tears running down her cheeks. "You've built your own prison. You refuse to believe in the good and choose to hang on to the bad instead You refuse to let people in, people that care, people who want to be a part of your life." Adelyn pushed the metal chair back from the table and stood. "Well, fine. If that's the way you want it, fine. If you won't let me in, that's your choice, but I am tired of this back-and-forth thing you keep doing." She raked her fingers across her forehead and pushed the hair away from her face. "I thought we might could be . . . something, friends at least." Her voice lowered, the fight leaving as quickly as it had come. "I guess I was wrong."

CHAPTER NINETEEN

idney watched the door shut behind Adelyn. She didn't understand. What he was afraid of happening was happening. She was just too nice, too good to see it. His behavior had caused her to come down to the police station tonight. The mother of a four-year-old, a second-grade teacher, had no business visiting a man in jail, especially a man brought in for fighting.

He reached up and touched his face where her hand had stroked his skin. The warmth of her touch had almost been too much. He had almost pulled her into his arms, almost given in to the longing to hold her close and tell her he would somehow be the man she needed him to be. If anything had been made clear to him today, though, it was what he had always felt, always known. He was not meant to be a father, a husband. Adelyn and Hazie May both deserved someone who could bring stability into their life, not drama. Someone who could protect them from their past without turning to violence to do it.

He leaned forward, elbows resting on the table, hands pressing against his face. This was for the best. Adelyn was mad. She would go home and calm down, see that he was right to push her away, that she was better off without him. The door squeaked opened and Sidney looked up. The officer stared into the room, waiting for Sidney to stand and follow him back to his cell.

"All right Alligator Man. Let's do this one more time." Sidney stepped through the door in front of the officer. "If all the inmates had as much company as you, we'd have to hire more help."

"Don't worry. That's everybody that will be coming." Sidney trudged down the hall and stepped into the cell. He waited for the door to lock shut behind him.

"Be thankful, man. Most people don't get visitors. At least you have people that care about you."

Sidney stepped into the gray visiting room again for the fourth time that evening. Langston had come after that weird visit from Adelyn's mother, telling him he would make sure Adelyn and Hazie May were okay at the apartment. Vivian and Fiona had come with Langston. Sidney was able to talk to them separately for only a few minutes each. Vivian was doing what needed to be done to get him out of jail. He would be back home tomorrow. Callie had called Fiona in a panic. The video and the flapping tongues in Carson's Bayou had spread his little soap opera around the town like wildfire. People were filling in the details of the little drama as they saw fit. Facts didn't matter. Fiona assured their little sister that Sidney was not buying or selling drugs, nor had he gone off the deep end and had a mental breakdown.

Shortly after they left, Adelyn showed up. After her visit, all he could do was lie on the cot and replay everything she said. It was a good thing he was in jail for the night. At least there, he didn't have to answer too many questions. In jail, he wasn't tempted to drive by the apartment and make sure Adelyn and Hazie May were okay, or drive through town and try to find out what Deborah Swan was up to. Zane Jones was still in jail. The deputy told him when he brought his supper. Since he broke a restraining order, he was in a lot of trouble. Adelyn and Hazie May were safe from the ex-husband.

Who was it this time? Could he refuse to see people? The squeaky metal door swung open, and Sidney's eyes stretched wide in surprise. "Pastor Connors." His preacher walked in wearing gym shorts and a Carson's Bayou Gators tee-shirt. "You didn't have to come down here to see me."

"I didn't have to, Sidney, but I wanted to." The preacher sat in the metal chair like he was sitting down in a lawn chair to chat with an old friend. "I've heard some wild stories and seen the video. Now I need you to tell me what really happened. Are Adelyn and Hazie May okay?"

"Langston checked on them. He said they are fine." Sidney looked across the table at his preacher. He listened to Pastor Connor's sermons and teachings every week. He spoke to him often at church and occasionally around town. The man had been a tremendous help to him and his sisters when Nana died, but he'd never dreamed he would see him in a scenario like this. In a position where he was the one needing the help. "I guess I should start from the beginning."

"I know you are dating Adelyn."

"No, not dating," Sidney said, leaning away from the table crossing his arms over his chest. "I mean." His eyes roamed around the blank grey walls then returned to the pastor. "She's staying in the apartment, and we eat our meals together, and go to church together and . . ." Sidney's voice trailed off. "Let me just start over and tell you the entire story."

"I think that's a good idea."

Once Sidney started telling Pastor Connors about Adelyn, how he found her on the side of the road that day a few months ago, how he let her stay in his apartment while he stayed in his rundown house, the whole story simply tumbled from his lips. He left nothing out, purging himself of all the guilt he felt for letting her down when she needed him, of all the fear of trying to be the man he needed to be for her, even though he was certain he would never measure up. "And now, here I am in jail. She's on her own again, and I'm stuck in a jail cell for the first time ever in my life."

"Sounds like you have gone through a lot together." Pastor Connors looked Sidney in the eye, holding his gaze.

"We have—she has. I've tried to be there, to help her, but I usually end up letting her down as much or more than I do helping her."

"I disagree."

"I lost Hazie May at the park," Sidney said, a frown pulling his mouth down. "Lost her. She could have followed that dog into the water and drowned. I didn't show up at the lawyer's office like I promised, and now." Sidney pressed the palms of his hands to the sides of his head. "Now I'm in jail for acting like a juvenile delinquent at the elementary school. Worse yet, I did it in front of her child. Pastor, I don't mean to argue, but those are not good things."

"Why were you watching the child that day at the park?" Pastor Collins continued to look at Sidney, voice calm.

"She needed to go see her parents. I was the only person here she knew, and she asked me to."

"Why were you planning on going to the law office with her?"

"It was going to be a hard day for her. She needed

someone there. She needed help to figure out how to handle getting the child support from her ex. I volunteered."

"And she wanted you there?"

"Yes, she did, but I wasn't there."

"And today?" A smile tugged at the corner of Pastor Connor's lips. "I've known you quite a while, Sidney. This is the first time I've ever seen you in anything besides blue jeans or coveralls. Today, you were in an alligator suit strolling around the school like you do those sorts of things all the time."

"Hazie May needed someone to be the alligator. She asked me. Adelyn couldn't do it, so I said I would. When her ex showed up and took Hazie May, I let my temper get the better of me and punched him."

"Look, Sidney, here's the thing. I've been listening to you for the past hour talk about you and Adelyn. What I am hearing is that Adelyn is coming to you for help with her problems, and you are doing your best to help her." Pastor Connors laid his hands on the table, palms up. "Is that right?"

"Yes." Sidney nodded. "I try to help, but I keep messing up. I'm not good at this kind of stuff. I'm good at cars, mechanical things, things I understand. Not relationships. Not people."

"Join the crowd, Sidney. We are all fumbling through. I think God sometimes lets us fail so we will learn to lean on Him instead of ourselves. Sometimes—most of the time, in a relationship where you are doing your best—it's as important to keep showing up and trying as it is to get it right."

"But what if I really mess things up?" Sidney stared down at his hands for several seconds, then lifted his eyes. "You know how my parents did me and my sisters. What if I'm like them?"

"First of all, from what your grandmother said before she passed away, and then Fiona, your parents were not Christians. They were living their lives to please themselves. You and your sisters were not their priority. You are a Christian, Sidney. I feel I know you fairly well. You have not done everything you've been doing over the past few months because there was some kind of personal gain in it for you. You did things like give up your brand-new apartment, give up your time, go out of your way to make sure this woman and her child were protected, and had what they needed. You need to ask yourself if these are things a selfish man would do."

"Most people would have done the same thing."

"No, Sidney, they wouldn't. Chances are, you were not the first vehicle that passed by Adelyn that day on the side of the road; however, you were the first one to stop. God placed that woman and her child in your life. Now you need to ask yourself why. Did he put her there so you can show her the love of Christ, be there for her when she needs you? Or did he put you there to tuck tail and run, to play it safe because you are scared of failure?"

"That's a lot to think about." Sidney looked past the pastor to the door, his voice quiet. "I guess it's a good thing I'm going to be in a place with no distractions for the next few hours."

"Sometimes God has to put us in some unusual situations to get our attention. Remember, wherever He puts us, He promises to be right there with us." Pastor Connors smiled. "Remember, Sidney, Adelyn keeps asking for your help. She obviously sees something in you, even when you don't. I've seen you two together. I think she cares for you a lot. You need to decide how you feel about her, what you want from this relationship. You then need to get over yourself and let God work through you to be who you are supposed to be."

"Ouch." Sidney looked at Pastor Connors and smiled. "You aren't pulling any punches."

"The truth stings sometimes, but we still need to hear it. You seem to be determined to compare yourself to the bad guys, like this ex-husband of Adelyn's, and your father. You are not the bad guy. Everybody seems to know this but you. It's time for you to open your hard-headed eyes and see it for yourself. Now, let's pray."

The deputy returned Sidney to his cell. He stretched out on the cot and stared at the ceiling. Everything they talked about swirled around in his head. Even though Adelyn said she wanted to just be friends and was taking steps to get a place of her own, she still spent all of her time with him. She came down to the garage where he was working; she asked his opinions. She shared her days with him.

He loved her. That was one thing he knew for sure. If she loved him, if she was willing to put herself out there for him, he would be there. He would put himself out there for her. He would keep showing up, like the preacher said. It was time to quit feeling sorry for himself and be the man she needed.

Did she love him? Was it possible she loved him? She was his friend and obviously cared, but love. There was so much to think about, so much to consider. He was not like his father. He could have been before Christ changed him, but he wanted, no, he longed to be the man God expected him to be. The fear of failure, his constant companion for so long, melted away. Peace washed over him like a warm bath after an eternity of stumbling around in a dry desert. *I can do all things through Christ who strengthens me.* A soft smile played on Sidney's lips in the dim light coming from the hallway. Paul had also been in jail when he wrote those words.

He would talk to Adelyn tomorrow. Explain to her about

the fight, why he had punched her ex right there in front of Hazie May. He might have gotten the child away from Zane Jones without violence, but at the time, getting her away before the man drove off had been the only thought in his brain. *Lord, guide my steps in this, in all I do. I'm leaning on You. I know I can't continue this relationship with Adelyn on my own. I'll mess it up. Guide my mind, my heart, my actions. I love her. I want to show up, be there always for her. I know that now. I'm ready.*

Sidney's eyes crept shut and pictures of Adelyn and Hazie May filled his head. Images of them dancing in the garage, playing with Peter in the backyard behind the apartment, eating ice cream at the park, all floated through his head. The good outweighed the bad. It wasn't even close. He wanted more of the good, even if it meant risking the mess-ups, the bads. If they were together, prayed up and seeking God, they could make it through the bads. That was certain.

CHAPTER TWENTY

"*I* know there's a reason why you were in Carson's Bayou." Adelyn stared across the coffee table at her mother. "I have a lawyer looking into everything, and I will hire a private investigator if I have to."

"You came here seeking me out," Deborah Swan said, raising an eyebrow. "You rekindled our relationship, Adelyn, not me. I did a little looking into your background. I admit that. When I found out about my granddaughter, I decided I needed to meet her." Adelyn's mother leaned back on the sofa and crossed her thin arms over her chest. "It's a good thing I have reinserted myself into your life. It's very obvious to me that you need help. Really, dear." She rolled her eyes. "An auto mechanic punching out your poor husband. What a scandal. I can't believe you are living with this man right in front of your own child."

"First of all." Adelyn's eyes narrowed. What were the words from the sermon earlier today about forgiving others when they trespassed against you? "I am not living with Sidney. I am renting the apartment above his garage from him. He has a house." She watched a condescending smile cross her mother's lips. "I don't care if you believe me or not, Mother, but I know you are up to something. The fact that my ex-husband happened to show up in town and tried to take my daughter on the same day that you showed up in town is too much of a coincidence to believe. Did you tell him where I was?"

"You came to me wanting help. Did you expect me to not look into things when you show up after five years? Besides, he's the father of your child, and he is a lot more respectable than the man you are hanging around with now."

"Did he tell you that there is a restraining order out against him, Mother?" Adelyn's jaw clenched. "Did he tell you I finally got up the nerve to leave him because he hit me right after I brought Hazie May home from the hospital? It took a while. I endured what he dished out for three years, Mother. Three more years of cowering and covering bruises before I saved up enough to hire a lawyer. I finally got the courage to walk away and had to endure another year of fighting to keep my child, trying to prove he was not the perfect man everyone saw." She watched the smugness on her mother's features fade. "Now, tell me what's going on. If you don't tell me now, I'll find out what you are up to, and when I do, I will put a stop to it. That is a promise."

"Don't get worked up." Deborah Swan ran her pointer finger along the edge of her perfectly lined lips. "I am looking out for your best interest—and Hazel's." She reached down and straightened a copy of Southern Living on the coffee table. "Your father's will left you a small sum of money, twenty thousand dollars. I was just trying . . ."

"Money?" Adelyn's mouth dropped open. "Why am I surprised? Of course, this is about money. But why didn't you tell me this when I was here before? Why were you in Carson's Bayou? Why in the world did you offer to be

Sidney's lawyer?" Adelyn tilted her head down and stared at her mother. "What are you up to?"

"I contacted your husband."

"Ex-husband."

"Your ex-husband," Deborah said, waving her hand in the air. "When you left the house that day, after reappearing out of the blue, I was in shock from seeing you after all these years. It took a while, and a few sessions with my therapist, but I finally got to thinking. I decided the best thing to do was to track you down and give you the money. I spoke with your father's lawyer. Yes, I contacted your ex-husband after our meeting at the coffee shop. You wouldn't tell me what was going on, why you shacked up with a grease monkey, so I called your ex. You just disappeared five years ago, then reappeared a few months ago. I did what I had to do. It turned out that your father had tracked you down. He knew you were married and living in Shreveport. I read through some of his papers and got the name of your ex-husband. I called him, and he told me you had left him."

"Daddy knew where I was?" Adelyn's shoulders slumped against the chair. "I wonder why he never contacted me?"

"You knew where we were. You never contacted us."

A cold blanket of grief wrapped around Adelyn. She stared ahead, her eyes not seeing her mother. "You're right. I should have gotten in touch with him." The room was silent as a tomb. Adelyn mourned not getting to talk with her father, not letting him see his grandchild, not seeing him at least one more time before he died.

"Your hus . . . ex-husband called Friday and said you were living with this mechanic. That's why I was there yesterday. I was planning on seeing you, talking some sense into your head, then I heard your name being thrown around at that little dive where I was eating." Deborah Swan raised her chin and glared at Adelyn with steely eyes. "Really. Fighting in the street in front of the school?" She slowly shook her head. "I went to the jail to help you, to try to save at least an ounce of your dignity and get the mechanic out of jail."

Adelyn blinked several times, focusing on what she had heard. Mother was not trying to help her. She didn't care what the woman was up to. "Keep the money." She stood from the chair. "I'm doing fine on my own, Mother. If you want to meet Hazie May, call me. I will introduce you on my terms, but don't go poking around in my life behind my back. Don't contact my ex-husband again." She looked her mother in the eye. "And stay away from Sidney."

"That's it?" Deborah Swan stood from the sofa, her jaw clenched. "No, thank you for trying to help me, Mother? No, I'm sorry I cut you out of my life for all these years, Mother? You're just leaving again?"

"Yes. I am." Adelyn bit her lower lip and looked at the woman, who hadn't said a kind word to her in so long that she couldn't recall it. "I am building a new life with people who love me and care about me. Not because they have to, or because I have some sort of status, but because they are good people, Godly people. Like I said, I will let you meet Hazie May. But I will not let you do to her what you did to me. Goodbye."

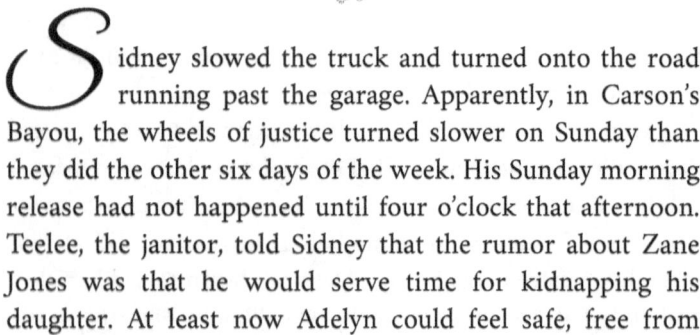

Sidney slowed the truck and turned onto the road running past the garage. Apparently, in Carson's Bayou, the wheels of justice turned slower on Sunday than they did the other six days of the week. His Sunday morning release had not happened until four o'clock that afternoon. Teelee, the janitor, told Sidney that the rumor about Zane Jones was that he would serve time for kidnapping his daughter. At least now Adelyn could feel safe, free from worrying about her ex bothering her or Hazie May anymore.

He pulled his truck into the gravel parking area in front of the garage and looked at the dark building. The tow truck was parked in its usual spot beside the garage office door, but Adelyn's little white car was nowhere to be seen. Sidney climbed out of his truck and walked to the stairs along the side of the garage leading to the apartment.

"Yeow." Peter's long, mournful call came from under the bottom step. Sidney squatted down, retrieving the cat from its hiding place. "Are they really gone?" He climbed the steps to the apartment, scratching the bony cat's chin as he hurried up the stairs. He turned the doorknob. Locked. The key was on the ring in his pocket, but it didn't seem right to go in without knowing whether Adelyn was still staying there or not. "They wouldn't just up and leave without saying good-bye, would they, boy?" Sidney scratched the cat behind the ears and headed back down the steps. She was furious last night, said she was done with him.

Even if she was leaving the apartment to get away from him, she wouldn't uproot Hazie May from school, or leave her new job. No, she was too smart for that. She was still somewhere in Carson's Bayou. He would find out where. No more waiting around or watching to see what would happen before he made a decision, that Sidney Madison was gone. He would find her and tell her how he felt. If she refused to listen to him today, he would come back tomorrow, and the next day if needed. They belonged together. It was so clear now. He just had to show her. He punched her cell number on his phone, but the call went straight to voicemail. After the way he treated her last night, he wasn't surprised. He would talk to her, though, that was certain.

Sidney slid back behind the wheel of his truck and turned the key. First things first. Run home and get a shower and change clothes. Sweat and jail cell were not a pleasant combination. After that, he would run over to Fiona's and see if she knew where Adelyn had gone.

"It's spooky looking, Momma." Hazie May's eyes stretched wide as their car pulled up in front of the run-down old house.

Adelyn looked again at the address on her phone screen. This was the right place, the address Fiona had given her, but was Sidney really living here? The grass was knee high, and the front porch looked like it was going to cave in any minute. Was Sidney staying here so she could live in his apartment?

"Sid!" Hazie May squealed and pointed to the front porch. "He's here, Momma. Sid lives in the spooky house. Hurry, Momma, undo my seatbelt."

Adelyn watched Sidney step through the dilapidated screen door, a towel draped around his shoulders, hair curling and damp. Yes, he must live here. She opened her car door and stepped to the back door to help Hazie May from her booster seat. "We decided to stop by for a visit," she called across the yard. "Is that okay?" After the way they left things last night, how would he receive her today? After church this morning, and then riding back from her mother's, something had become clear. She could not force Sidney Madison to be someone he was not, but she could accept him for who he was. If he only wanted to be a friend, even a distant friend, she would take that. She couldn't tear down the walls around his heart, only he could do that with the help of the Lord. She wouldn't abandon him though. She cared for him too much to do that. He cared too. He had to, and however long it took him to figure it out, she would wait.

Sidney stepped off the bottom stair and scooped Hazie May into a hug as she barreled into his arms. Yes, she would wait forever if she had to for that man.

"Do you really live here, Sid?" Hazie May looked past Sidney's shoulder to the house behind him. "Do ghosts live with you?"

"Hazie May." Adelyn walked across the tall grass to the saggy porch steps to where Sidney waited. "There's no such thing as ghosts and you are being rude."

"Yes, I live here," Sidney said, glancing at Adelyn. He smiled down at Hazie May, "and no. There are no ghosts. Just me."

"Can we go in and look around?" Hazie May leaned toward the front door. "Do you have 'lectricity?"

"Why yes I do, and yes we can." Sidney raised an eyebrow at Hazie May. "Want a Yoo-hoo?"

"You bet." Hazie May smiled and wiggled out of Sidney's arms.

Sidney tugged on the screen door, forcing it open as it scraped across the porch floor. He stepped to the side as Adelyn followed Hazie May inside. "I guess the place has really gone down since Fiona and Callie moved out, but I'm not here much, anyway. You want a Coke?"

"No. I'm good." Adelyn watched Sidney pull a Yoo-hoo from an ice chest sitting in the doorway leading to the kitchen. He must have moved his refrigerator to the apartment. She looked at the couch sitting against the wall of the living room and the old recliner on the other wall. "Is this where you grew up?"

"Yes. This is my Nana's old place. Callie has the TV with her, and the fridge is at the apartment, but I have everything I need here."

"What's that bucket for?" Hazie May looked at them both, a brown mustache on her upper lip from her Yoo-hoo. "Is that where you water your dog?"

"No." Sidney stepped over and picked up the pot from the floor near the front door. "The roof sometimes leaks. I should have picked that old pot up already."

"Sidney. We need to talk." Adelyn looked around the room. He had given her the best of everything he owned and stayed in a place that was falling down around his ears. "Some things have got to change."

CHAPTER TWENTY-ONE

"So, you've been sleeping in a little twin bed and keeping things cool in an ice chest while I sleep in your bed and live in your apartment?" Adelyn stared into Sidney's face, her eyes shining brightly. "I've never had anyone," she paused, rubbing her lips together, searching for the right words. "No one has ever cared enough for me to make sacrifices the way you have." She looked across the park where Hazie May was playing on the slides with a boy about her size, both children laughing and carefree. Her gaze drug away from her daughter and back to Sidney's waiting face, his eyes watching her expectantly. "You put my needs ahead of your own. I mean, I knew you were going out of your way to help me, but you've given up a lot for me. Much more than I imagined. I don't know how to thank you."

"I don't need a thank you." Sidney looked down into Adelyn's face. "I've always known something was missing from my life, that I wanted what Fiona and Langston and so many other people my age have, but until I found you that day on the side of the road, I didn't have the courage to pursue that missing piece." A bark of laughter caught in his throat. "Who am I kidding? Until last night after that talk with the preacher, I still didn't have the courage."

"The preacher? What did he say?"

"Well, he sort of said that I needed to either ride the horse or get out of the saddle. God had given me a great opportunity by letting you come into my life, and I was messing it up by pushing you away."

"Hallelujah, and pass the ketchup." Adelyn's eyes sparkled, and her face split into a grin. "Remind me to thank the man next time I see him." The laughter faded as a soft smile settled on her face. "You are so worried about the baggage you are bringing to the table that you are overlooking my baggage. I have a lot of baggage: a crazy ex-husband, a slightly psycho mother, and, don't forget, I'm a penniless beggar with emotions all over the map." She reached up and brushed a brown curl back from Sidney's forehead. "I'm not perfect. I understand that you're not perfect, but the fact is, we are both so much better when we're together."

"I know." Sidney placed his hand over Adelyn's, sliding it down to his cheek. "I can't promise you that I will get everything right. I can't promise that I will have all the answers. But after last night, I can promise one thing. If you will take me, I will be here—I'll be here as a friend, as a boyfriend, however you will accept me." He tilted his face to the side, turning his lips to her palm. "I love you, Adelyn. I always will."

The softness of Sidney's lips brushed against her palm and a shiver ran up Adelyn's arm. "I love you too," she whispered, choking back the tears threatening to rise to the surface. She leaned closer, and Sidney's other hand found the back of her head as he drew her mouth toward his lips. This kiss. This was how it was supposed to be. Any doubt, any worry Adelyn may have harbored somewhere in the back of her mind about committing herself to another man floated away as Sydney's lips gently found hers.

"Mother said Daddy left me twenty thousand dollars in his will." Adelyn looked across the shiny cherry wood desk at Vivian. "She said that's why she came back to Carson's Bayou when Sidney was in jail a couple of weeks ago. She wanted to give me the money when she found out I had a child to support."

"I hate to talk ugly about your mother." Vivian slid a paper across the desk for Adelyn to look at. "But your mother was lying. According to his will, he left half of the life insurance money to your mother and half to you. She should have told you about this immediately after your father's death."

"My mother is not a good person, but I really don't think she knew where I was when my father died. She said that my father discovered I was living in Shreveport, but she didn't find out he knew this, or where I was, until I came to see her after I moved to Carson's Bayou."

"Well." Vivian drew her eyebrows together. "I'm afraid that's not true. The will stated that if you refused the money or did not take possession of the money after five years, your portion would go to your mother as well. All of this information was in the same document, with instructions on how to reach you. Apparently, your father kept pretty close tabs on you through the years. There's also a significant amount of money set aside in an account for your daughter for college. This money goes to her even if you turn down your father's allotment of the will."

Adelyn shook her head and sighed. "I shouldn't be surprised. Mother always has some kind of motive for everything she does that benefits her in some way. When is the five years up? Or is it already up? Probably not if Mother was offering to give me the twenty thousand dollars. She knew I would find out about the money soon, anyway."

"Oh, the amount is a lot higher than twenty thousand." Vivian reached across the desk and pointed to a highlighted figure on the papers. "The five years ends November thirtieth, just a couple of weeks from now."

"One-hundred-eighty-thousand dollars?" Adelyn looked at the paper, and her eyes stretched wide. "It's starting to make sense why she contacted my ex-husband and then went to the jail to see Sidney." Adelyn slumped back against the leather chair, and her eyes wandered around the room. "She was either trying to get me back with my ex-husband, so I would not reach out to her again, or keep my life in chaos so I would not start looking into Daddy's affairs. Whatever it took to keep me out of the way, or under her thumb to control me until the expiration date had passed so she could keep all the money. How come I am just now hearing about his will? Shouldn't someone have contacted me about all of this before?"

"Your mother is a lawyer, remember? I'm sure she took responsibility for contacting you. It's perfectly reasonable to assume that she would have informed you of everything since she's your mother. You need to talk to the life insurance company in the next few days to straighten everything out, but I imagine you will find out that they were told you didn't want anything to do with your father's will or the inheritance."

"Can you help me do that?"

"Sure. I will contact the agency and set up a meeting before the expiration date." Vivian leaned back in her chair. "Do you mind if I make a suggestion?"

"No, of course not."

"I understand things are not good between you and your mother, but you should take this money." Vivian smiled politely. "Then you can go ahead and get you and your daughter a place to live. You won't have to wait on Lucas and the housing committee from the ministry. The reason I'm saying this is because another family, an elderly couple raising their three grandkids, just lost their house in a fire. They are all staying at the shelter until they can find a more permanent solution. The old couple is on a fixed income, and their options for rebuilding are slim, practically nonexistent. If you contact the committee to withdraw your request for the house, they can go ahead and start on this one, rebuilding where their old house was." Vivian tucked a strand of black hair behind her ear and looked at Adelyn. "I realize this is really none of my concern, but I feel I know you well enough to tell you this. Of course, whatever you decide about the money and the house and everything is completely up to you. What I just said will never be mentioned outside of these doors. The housing ministry agreed to build you the house. I feel they will stand by that obligation even if your circumstances change."

"Oh man. Um." Adelyn's lips pushed into a thin line as what Vivian said sunk in. "I will definitely let the other family build the house. I have a place to stay even if I don't take the money, and since our engagement, Sidney and I were thinking it wouldn't be right to take the help anyway. Once we are married next year, we will be able to live in the apartment together or find another place without outside help. You can tell your husband I am withdrawing my application for a house. I will do whatever I need to do to make that official."

Adelyn looked down at the papers sitting on the desk in front of her, then slowly lifted her eyes. "If I take this money, are there any stipulations? Like, will my mother gain any type of hold over me, or will we be in some kind of contract together since we both received money from my father's will? If that's the case, I don't want the money."

"No." Vivian punched a button on the keyboard in front of her and looked at the computer screen to her right. "The life insurance company will give you the money, and that's a done deal. As far as the money for your daughter, neither you nor your mother can do anything with that. It becomes the child's when she is eighteen. They will give it to her in allotments twice a year for six years."

"Okay." Adelyn pulled in a deep breath of air and blew it out through pursed lips. "Go ahead and contact whoever you need to contact. I will talk to Sidney about all of this. We have already discussed the housing thing. We were planning on letting your husband and the housing committee know about giving back the house at their meeting next week. This just kind of puts a new spin on things."

"Is that the ring?" Vivian looked at Adelyn's hand as she ran her fingers through the top of her hair. "Can I see?"

"Oh, of course." Adelyn held her left hand out to show Vivian the half carat solitaire diamond ring. "I told Sidney I didn't need a ring when he asked me to marry him, but he insisted."

"It's beautiful. When did he propose?"

"This past Sunday at the park." Adelyn looked down at the ring and laughed. "Hazie May almost let the cat out of the bag before church, but Sidney was able to hush her up before I figured anything out. We got ice cream cones and walked to the bench to watch her play on the merry-go-round, but she wouldn't go play. She just kept standing there. I figured something was up. When he pulled out the ring box, Hazie May started spinning around and singing about getting married and weddings before he could even open the box and ask me."

"That sounds just about perfect." Vivian bit her lower lip. A grin crept across her face. "I must admit that Fiona and I are so excited to have you in our little family. We aren't exactly kin, but Langston and Fiona kind of have a way of bringing everyone they love into their family circle. It is going to be so fun to have your daughter at Thanksgiving. We will celebrate it at Fiona and Langston's house this year. Next year, Lucas and I will have it at our house."

"I am so blessed." Adelyn's cheeks flushed, her eyes glistening with unshed tears. "Last year at Thanksgiving, it was me and Hazie May in a little apartment with no other family at all, eating Chinese takeout. This year we will be surrounded by family, and from what I understand, all kinds of great food."

"Definitely no takeout boxes on Thanksgiving this year."

CHAPTER TWENTY-TWO

*A*delyn followed Sidney through the kitchen of Nana's old house and out onto the back porch, the rusty screen door bumping shut behind them. A tire swing hanging from an enormous oak tree near the back-yard fence swayed slightly in the fall breeze, damp brown leaves scattering the ground below. The grass, just as deep in the backyard as the front, grew up around two rusty old cars sitting on blocks. She looked to the side, and the tail of another junked out car was around the corner edge of the house.

"Okay." Sidney draped his arm around Adelyn's shoulders. "That's the grand tour. Ready to head back to Fiona's and get Hazie May?"

"No, not yet." Adelyn stepped over to the edge of the back porch and placed her hand on the post by the steps. "I want to talk to you about something that's on my mind. Can we sit down a minute?"

"Sure." Sidney watched Adelyn sit down on the cracked concrete steps. "Let me grab us a bottle of water from the ice chest. I'll be right back."

Adelyn looked along the back of the porch, waiting for Sidney to return. An old seven-sister rose bush looked more like a briar patch than a rose. It wandered haphazardly along a rotting wooden trellis leaning against the back of the house on the far side of the porch, completely out of control and in dire need of pruning. A sagging clothesline hung between two metal T-shaped poles near a rickety wooden fence on the other side of the porch. This place must have looked so cute and homey years ago when Sidney and his sister were small, and his grandmother tended the rose bush and cared for the home.

"Here you go." Sidney eased down beside Adelyn and handed her a cold water bottle, wet from sitting in the melting ice. "Now. What's on your mind?"

"This is where I want to live." Adelyn turned shining eyes toward Sidney. "I want to take the money Daddy left me and fix this place up. I want to raise Hazie May, and the future children we are going to have right here where you grew up."

"Here?" Sidney's forehead wrinkled. "I don't know." His eyes roamed around the overgrown yard and back to the rundown house behind him. "Maybe we could tear this place down and just build a new house on this lot."

"No, Sidney. I know you can't see it, but I can. We can talk to Lucas and Langston, find out if it can be done. We can close in this back-porch area and make it our bedroom, then add a wraparound porch. That will give us three bedrooms for the kids. If that's not enough, we will add more rooms as the family grows. This will be a beautiful place once we haul the junk off and renovate the house. Of course, we will need to keep enough money back to get a decent lawn mower. I take it yard work is not your thing."

"First of all, how many kids are we having?" Sidney asked, suppressing the grin taking over his face. "And second, those cars are not junk. They are future projects. And third, no, I don't love to mow, but I will if I'm going to have a brood of little ones running around the place."

"Well. You own a shop with plenty of field behind it for all of your future projects." Adelyn leaned her head over on Sidney's shoulder. "Will you at least think about it? I want to have roots. I want our house to have character, to be a part of who we are. Living here where you grew up will be wonderful. I know you will need to talk to your sisters, see if they are okay with us moving in here and changing the house where they grew up, but will you at least consider it?"

"There's nothing to consider." Sidney leaned over and touched his lips to the top of Adelyn's head. "If this is where you want us to live, then this is where we will live. I'm sure Fiona and Callie will be fine with it. Callie says this place needs a wrecking ball taken to it. She won't care as long as nobody is asking her to live here. Fiona will be happy that we are saving the place."

"I'm so glad God sent that deer into the road that day I was headed to my parents' house. If He hadn't, I would have never ended up in the ditch and never met you."

"His ways are not our ways. Aren't you glad?"

"Yes, future husband of mine. Very Glad."

If you enjoyed this book, please take a few minutes to leave a review now. Authors, myself included, really appreciate this, and it helps draw more readers to books they may enjoy as well. Thanks! KC

Sign up for KC"s newsletter and receive a free eBook copy of Music Smarts and Wounded Hearts

Please keep reading for a sneak peek of book four in the Carson's Bayou series, Callie Madison's story.

Read People Smarts and Wounded Hearts

PEOPLE SMARTS AND WOUNDED HEARTS

*C*allie Madison leaned forward and twirled the red straw through her iced white chocolate mocha coffee, staring across the table at her sister. "It's not like I'm asking you to give me the money. It's a loan. I'll pay it back when I graduate, with interest." She rubbed her lips together and the sweet chocolate flavor of her coffee mixed with the berry flavor of her lip gloss. "I just don't see what the big deal is. I thought you wanted me to go to college to better myself. I mean, if you think about it, I'm doing this as much for you as I am for myself."

Fiona raised her piping hot black coffee to her lips and blew the swirl of rising steam from the cup. She stared at her younger sister's bouncy blond curls, pulled away from her face with a baby blue headband. The polka dots on the head band matched the blue and white striped tank top that clung to Callie's perfectly toned figure like a well-fitting glove. Her tanned legs, crossed at the knee, emerged from the blue jean mini skirt and continued down to the flashy red toenails showing from the rhinestone studded flip flops. These nails matched the manicured nails now drumming the tabletop as her baby sister looked at her, eyes stretched wide. "Cal, this is not easy for me to say, and I think you know it. It's not that we don't want you to have the money, and I do want you to finish your education. But it took you four years to finish a two-year junior college. Not because you don't have the brains, because we both know that's not the case. You just started putting other things, like parties and dating and whatever, ahead of studying." Fiona blew out a deep breath of air and took a sip of the coffee. "We're thinking that if you work for a year, save up your money to put toward the tuition, that you will start taking your education seriously."

"You're not being fair." Callie leaned back in the wooden chair and looked around the Bayou Bean, careful to keep her voice low. A couple of girls she had graduated from junior college with back at the beginning of the summer sat a few tables over, near the picture window facing the busy street. Wouldn't they love to know that all the bragging she had done about leaving Carson's Bayou and going to LSU this fall was falling flat? One of the girls, Bridget, the plump one that loved to gossip, looked over her shoulder to where Callie and Fiona sat, the nosy little pigeon. Callie stretched her lips into a broad smile and nodded in Bridget's direction, making sure their eyes met and held. Bridget jerked her head back around, caught in the act of spying. Callie turned her gaze back to Fiona. "I had a heavy load with the volleyball practice, and then all the debate team meetings. It was too much to keep on top of. Besides, college is supposed to make you a well-rounded person. Part of the reason people go to college is for the social growth experience." Callie batted her eyes at her big sister. "I wasn't doing anything bad, Fi. I just couldn't keep up."

"Hogwash." Fiona set the coffee cup down on the table a little too hard. "Rich people might send their kids to colleges and universities for the social experience, but the rest of us go to learn something that will help us get a decent job and support ourselves for the rest of our lives." Her head cocked to the side, and she glared at her sister. "If you want social growth, go to the library and check out a few books. Do a little reading about the world. That will grow you way more than spending all your time with Dawson Wallace. Honestly, Callie, I don't know what you see in that guy."

"There's nothing wrong with Dawson." Callie raised her chin. "He's a sweet guy. He's not a Wade, but I wasn't lucky enough to fall for the richest guy in town." She looked down and rubbed the glossy red surface of the nails on her left hand with the fingers on her right. "You dropped out of college the first time you went." She slowly raised her eyes and looked at Fiona. "At least I kept going and graduated."

"See?" Fiona spat out the words like they were bad medicine. "That's the reason I'm not letting Langston give you a free ride to LSU. You know good and well that I dropped out to get married. It was stupid and Jeff was a jerk, but while I was there, I did the work and made the grades. I was working hard and saving all I could to go back to school until Nanna got sick . . ." Fiona's words faded. She reached her hand across the table, the anger vanishing as quickly as it came. Tears glistened in Callie's eyes as Fiona squeezed her hand. "I don't want to fight with you," she said, her voice becoming soft. "I'm not going to fight with you. The fact is, now I have a daughter of my own, and hopefully one day soon, Catherine will have a little brother or sister."

"You're pregnant?" A smile tugged at the corners of Callie's lips; the anger of a few seconds ago completely forgotten.

"Not yet." Fiona returned the smile. "But we're trying."

"Okay." Callie's shoulders slumped, and she sniffed back the unshed tears. "What do you want me to do?"

"Don't act like it's the end of the world." Fiona pulled her hand back and picked up her mug, the coffee's rich aroma floating up and urging her to continue. A chestnut strand of hair dropped from the pile of messy curls pulled to the back of her head. She brushed it out of the way and sipped her coffee. "Get a job. Save your money. You're living in Sidney's apartment and driving my Beetle. You should be able to save almost every penny if you don't." Fiona glanced down at Callie's manicured hands. "If you don't let it slip through your fingers. In a year, if you've worked hard and have part of the tuition, we will help you with the rest."

"Is that it? One year of work and then you help with school?"

"No." Fiona took a bigger sip of the cooling coffee then returned it to the table. "You also have to decide on a major. We won't help pay your tuition if you don't know what you are going to school for. But you have an entire year to think about it, so that shouldn't be a problem." Fiona looked down at her cell phone laying on the table. "Oh man, it's already two. I have to pick Catherine up from the sitter." She reached across the table again and squeezed Callie's hand. "Don't be mad at me. I hate it when we are mad at each other."

"I'm not mad." Callie pulled in a deep breath of air and huffed it out. "I'm ready to get through school and get out of this town. Another year stuck in Carson's Bayou is like a prison sentence."

"Well, put on your orange jumpsuit and get to work." Fiona stood from her chair, her gauzy ankle-length skirt draping around her willowy frame. "Your sentence will be over before you know it. There's a HELP WANTED sign over in the window." She nodded her head to the front of the coffee shop where Callie's friends sat. "You can probably start here tomorrow if you don't put me down as a reference."

"I don't know." Callie looked up at her tall, thin, perfect

big sister and winked. "Your antics at the Bayou Bean are legendary. I have a feeling simply having the name Madison will forever ban me from employment here.

*ope. Callie took out her cell phone and pulled up the help wanted section of the paper. She might have to work for a year, but she was not going to wait tables or hustle coffee out to her snobby friends. She had an associate degree from the junior college. Yes, it was a general studies degree with the minimum amount of math that she could get away with, but it was still a degree. There had to be something around here she could do besides being a food jockey.

She scrolled past the posting for a cashier at the dollar store and a stocker at the grocery store. She continued through the listing for private sitters for the elderly and daycare workers. "That looks promising." Callie pulled a drink of the sweet coffee concoction through her straw and read the post. Office manager needed for new business opening August first. Honor Systems Technology is looking for an office manager proficient in planning and organization, analysis and assessment, time management, and communication, multi-tasking and conflict resolution. This person will need to have a thorough understanding of billing clients and running a budget and be proficient in multiple prominent computer software programs.

The communication thing would not be a problem, or conflict resolution. She could talk her way out of any problem. The rest of the stuff on the list—that was another story.

Crash! Callie jerked her head toward the explosive sound in time to see the barista, a high school girl that probably weighed ninety pounds soaking wet, drop a tray with a couple of drinks and some pastries near the cash register. She turned her head away from the girl, and looked over at the help wanted sign in the window of the Bayou Bean. That was the job she was qualified for, but good grief. The two girls she graduated with were laughing, literally laughing out loud at the poor kid near the counter. The hyenas.

Callie got up and hurried to where the girl was kneeling, picking up the mess. "Here," she said, squatting beside her as she picked up the silverware and coffee mugs. "Let me help. Just ignore those biddies. They need to be taught a few manners."

"Thank you." The girl looked at Callie, near hero worship written all over her face. "These trays weigh a ton, and Mr. Randall will have a fit if he hears I spilled one."

Callie helped the poor kid get everything back on the tray, then returned to her table, refusing to look over near the window. She slid into her chair and looked back down at the list of requirements for the office manager. She had made a B in creative writing. Her resume might require a little bit of her creative touch, but she needed the office manager's job. Besides, she was twenty-two. She knew as much about computer software as any other likely candidate in Carson's Bayou. The place was not overflowing with technology geeks, after all.

Callie pushed her chair back and stood up, stretching her shoulders. She smiled at a couple of guys who looked her way as she headed out the door. She could get this job for sure if the person doing the interview was a dude, but she couldn't bank on that. No, she wouldn't actually lie on her resume, not really. She would be creative. Once she got the position, she would buckle down and figure out everything she needed to know. Fiona said she was smart, and Fiona knew her better than anybody. She could do this. One year of hard work, then bye-bye Carson's Bayou.

. . .

Buy People Smarts and Wounded Hearts on Amazon or read for free in Kindle Unlimited.

People Smarts and Wounded Hearts

Join KC's newsletter and receive the free eBook Music Smarts and Humble Hearts

ACKNOWLEDGMENTS

Thank you Lord for this story. For some reason, it was a little harder to write than the last two. Maybe it hit a bit closer to home for me? I don't know.

Sidney and Adelyn are both flawed people, just like the rest of us, but they learn to lean on God first and each other second. This is my prayer for me all the time, that I will always lean on my God first, then the wonderful spouse he gifted me all those years ago. I was a starry eyed girl and fell in love with Mr. Wonderful's deep voice, black curly hair, and unbelievably bright blue eyes. I'm so thankful the Lord led me to a godly man when I was looking at all the outer trimmings.

ABOUT THE AUTHOR

KC Hart is the author of inspirational romance and humorous southern cozy mysteries with a Christian world view. KC lives in Mississippi with Mr. Wonderful, her husband of thirty-eight years, where she spends her days enjoying the grandkids, reading, writing, and playing her piano or guitar. One of her favorite things to do is sit on the back porch in the evening and eat watermelon before the mosquitos come out to play.

All KC's books are free of foul language, sex and graphic gore. KC says you can leave her books on the coffee table when your momma or the preacher stops in for a visit and you won't have to blush.

KC asks that you pray for her as she crafts new stories. Her desire is that each story will point the reader to Christ.

If you enjoyed this book, please take a few minutes to leave a review now. Authors, myself included, really appreciate this, and it helps draw more readers to books they may enjoy as well. Thanks! KC

Sign up for KC's newsletter and receive the eBook Music Smarts and Humble Hearts

Follow KC on her social media platforms
https://www.bookbub.com/profile/kc-hart?list=
author_books

https://www.goodreads.com/author/show/20570083.
K_C_Hart

Dear Friends,

I wanted to let you know how much I appreciate the support you show me through the emails, social media posts, reviews, cards and letters. I have come to know so many of you through this type of contact and you have made my life richer.

I ask, as always, that you continue to pray for me as I write my stories. I am always reading books on how to improve my writing, but the one thing that is most important to me is to share the heart of Christ correctly and in a meaningful way to the reader. I feel this type of evangelism is what my writing is all about. I want my characters to pull people closer to the Lord with their stories and I want my stories to get into the hands of those that will enjoy them and those that need to see them. Again, thank you for all you do.

Blessings,

KC Hart

BOOKS BY KC HART

A Christmas Blaze

Fresh Starts and Small Town Hearts

Business Smarts and Reckless Hearts

Car Smarts and Bashful Hearts

People Smarts and Wounded Hearts

Kid Smarts and Wistful Hearts

Family Smarts and Runaway Hearts

Elsie: Prairie Roses Collection

Moonlight, Murder and Small Town Secrets

Music, Murder and Small Town Romance

Memories. Murder and Small Town Money

Merry Murder and Small Town Santas

Medicine Murder and Small Town Scandal

Marriage, Murder & Small Town Schemes

Mistaken Murder & Small Town Status

Mistletoe, Murder & Small Town Scoundrels